DOUBLE VISION

by

Ellie Hart

2019

DOUBLE VISION

ISBN 13: 978-1-63555-385-7

This Trade Paperback Original Is Published By
Bold Strokes Books, Inc.
P.O. Box 249
Valley Falls, NY 12185

First Edition: March 2019

Credits
Editor: Jerry L. Wheeler
Production Design: Stacia Seaman
Cover Design by Tammy Seidick

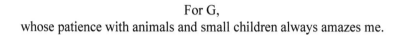
For G,
whose patience with animals and small children always amazes me.

Chapter One

I hate mornings. I was never a morning person like my sister, perky and ready for the day as soon as her eyes opened. I am the night owl of the family, better suited to activities performed under cover of darkness. I am more enamored with the sunset than the dawn, with the stars rather than the sun. And you can chalk it up to karma, fate, or payback, but I am in love with a lark.

The lark, however, is currently bent over the toilet, retching and moaning, cursing the day she decided to have a baby. I do my part, holding her head and handing her a glass of water, careful to keep my own nausea hidden. I am beyond elated we are going to be parents, but I am very glad she's the one carrying our child. I would have chickened out as soon as I realized what the physical commitment involved.

"Can you call in to work for me?" Marta's voice is muffled as she leans into her crossed arms, face hidden. "There's no way I can even drive this morning."

"Sure, babe." I pat her on the shoulder, glad to be doing something besides waiting for her to stagger back to bed. "Should I tell them you'll be out tomorrow as well?"

Marta's only response is a grunt, followed by the sound of dry heaving. The obstetrician has assured us this phase will pass, and I can hardly wait. Marta doesn't comment, at least not in words, whenever I try to encourage her. She's gotten good at conveying her thoughts with a look, and I've gotten good at understanding what she's trying to say, which is usually something along the lines of "get lost." I'm sure she means it with love.

I leave her and head back to our room. I need to call in for her before her boss has a fit. Marta is one of the best social workers employed by Alameda County, and the amount of work she takes on would amaze anyone else. It certainly puts the rest of her office in a pissy mood whenever she's gone. Just having to divvy up her caseload can send some of the less motivated employees ducking for cover.

My phone is ringing as I walk around the bed and stumble over the scuffed tennis shoes I dropped there the night before. Call it an atavistic response, but I always attempt to answer before it goes to voice mail. Why? I can't tell you. It's just one of my many idiosyncrasies Marta says she loves. When she's not pregnant, that is. Right now, anything I do can irritate her without rhyme or reason.

"Dr. Cutler," I say into the mouthpiece. I can hear the sound of frenzied barking in the background and have to grin. There's only one person who can be calling me from the veterinarian clinic I run. "What's up, buttercup?"

"Your butt on a platter, that's what's up. Did someone forget she promised to run the free clinic today?"

I groan. It's my turn to oversee the monthly clinic for pets belonging to the homeless population. When I first volunteered, I figured a couple hours a month, give or take, would be the extent of it. To my surprise, we had enough dogs and cats—and even a couple of ferrets and a hairless rat—to fill two days' worth of checkups, minor surgeries, and vaccinations.

"Lou, is there any chance you can get someone else to

fill in for me? Marta's tossing her cookies again, and I don't think I can leave her on her own today." I cross my fingers in a superstitions gesture. Dr. Louise Grafton, my partner at the clinic and an excellent vet in her own right, doesn't suffer fools gladly.

I hear Lou give a snort on the other end of the line, and I grimace. That's not a good indication.

"This'll make it three times this month, Giselle. You two should have known what you were getting into when you decided to go the natural route, you know?"

You're preaching to the choir. "Just chalk it up to newbies, Lou. So, whaddya say?"

"Fine." Her voice has softened a tad, the first suggestion of victory. I stop myself from giving a fist pump. "But I'm keeping score, girlie." She pauses, then adds in a much kinder tone, "Tell that woman of yours to sip ginger ale. That always helped me."

"I will," I say fervently, feeling as though I'd just taken down a brick wall with my bare hands. "And thanks, Lou. You're a gem among women."

Lou laughs into my ear, a hearty sound that makes me grin.

"And don't I know it. All right, Giselle. See ya when I see ya."

With that battle out of the way, it's time to tackle Marta's boss. She's not as understanding as Lou, not by a long shot. I try not to think negative thoughts about the woman, I really do, but she's never made it a secret how she feels about a child being raised by two women.

"We all know a child is better off with a mom and a dad," she's said before. "That's what every child needs."

That's where I stop listening and begin thinking of ways to hex her. Just kidding, of course. Kind of. I'm still carrying on an imaginary argument with her when the ringing on the other end of the line stops and her voice mail kicks in. Interesting. This is a woman who is never late, never misses a day of work, and certainly never misses a phone call.

I leave my message, telling the machine Marta Perry will not be at work today or tomorrow, and then disconnect before a live person picks up. I only have so much courage to go around, and right now it's all focused on the pregnant woman in my bathroom.

"Don't you think you might be a little old for this?" I asked Marta that nearly a year ago, just before a size seven loafer came sailing across the bedroom, hitting me squarely between the shoulders. I learned two things from that verbal faux pas: never assume a woman over forty is too old for anything, and never turn your back on said woman.

After that, I kept my thoughts to myself. However, as I lean against the doorframe to our master bathroom and watch her wash her pale face under the tap, I begin wondering once more exactly what we're getting into. Six more months of this, I think, not to mention the first eighteen years of the kiddo's life. That's a mighty long sentence for something I'm not even sure about.

"Did you call me in?" Marta turns to look at me, and I am struck by the new thinness of her face. I thought pregnant women were supposed to get, well, chubby, not look like someone who hasn't seen a good meal for a while. I make a mental note to call the doctor myself as I paste on a smile.

"That I did, love. And I bought you an extra day as well." I hold out one hand to her. "Let's get you back in bed, and I'll bring you some hot tea and toast, all right?"

Marta grunts in response, but she pauses next to me and winds her arms around my waist, leaning her head on my shoulder. I close my eyes and kiss the top of her head, careful not to hug her too tightly. This new Marta, the holy temple carrying a new life, feels frail underneath my own arms. You better be nice to your mama, I say silently to the baby. I've known her a lot longer than I've known you.

"So what did Lou want?" Marta raises her head so she can look into my face. "Let me guess: get your sorry ass to work."

"Something along those lines," I agree. "And how'd you know it was Lou on the phone?"

She rolls her eyes and untangles herself from my grasp.

"Are you going in?"

I follow her into the bedroom, watching her walk unsteadily toward the bed.

"Not a snowball's chance in hell," I say, pulling back the covers so she can climb in. "And she's already got someone to cover for me at the free clinic, so it's all good."

She pauses and looks at me over her shoulder, one eyebrow lifted slightly. "Is that today?"

I nod, motioning for her to get under the blankets. "I'll go tomorrow if they need me," I say, tucking the comforter around her feet. "It really depends on how many come to the clinic today."

Marta's hair, cropped short and dark against the white sham, is an art form unto itself. A gel-stiffened strand is bent in two, creating a small hook that looks like it belongs on top of a peacock's head. Her sideswept bangs nearly cover her eyebrows, and I reach over to push them back.

"No butter," she says, and I agree. I've always loved taking care of Marta, and this pregnancy has given me ample opportunities to show her how I feel.

"Dry toast and hot tea coming right up, love."

I smooth her hair back once more and head for the kitchen. It's a chef's dream in there, all stainless steel and granite, natural gas, and filtered water. Marta is the cook in this house, and I've missed her impromptu gourmet meals more than I let on. One can only stand so many pasta-based dishes, you know?

I'm just putting the bread into the toaster when my cell phone begins a maniacal rendition of "Bohemian Rhapsody," my latest ringtone choice. I don't recognize the number on the screen. The area code is local, though, so I punch the green icon and answer.

"Dr. Cutler."

"Is this Marta's roommate?"

I grit my teeth, tempted to hang up.

"Yes," I say, trying to sound halfway gracious. "How can I help you?"

"This is Chrissy Burton, Marta's supervisor."

Oh boy, I think. Here we go. I gird up my mental loins for battle.

"I've already called her in, Ms. Burton. Is there—"

"It's not about Marta," she says, her voice strident. "It's about me."

"Oh?" I can't help if it I sound a tad cynical. "Is there a message you'd like for me to pass along?"

To my amazement, I can hear muffled sobs in my ear. Chrissy Burton is crying.

"Dr. Cutler, I really need to talk to you." I hear her take in a shaky breath. "Please."

Behind me, the toast has popped up, ready to be plated. I tuck the cell phone between my ear and shoulder, my head at an awkward angle as I reach into a glass-fronted cabinet for a small dish.

"Is it about your pet?" I ask as I open a drawer under the gleaming stove, pulling out a cookie sheet I press into service as a tray. "I'm not on duty today, but Dr. Grafton is at the clinic."

"Pet? I don't have a pet," she says, a touch of snappishness underpinning her words. "As I've already said, this is about me."

"Ms. Burton," I say firmly as I assemble the bland breakfast, "I'm home today because my partner is very ill. Right now isn't a good time for a phone call, so if there's something you need to tell me, it needs to happen in the next minute or two. Please," I add, not really meaning it.

"I'm sorry." She sounds deflated, all the wind out of her verbal sails. "Would it be better if I call back in an hour or so?"

I make a snap decision, another one of my foibles Marta puts up with.

"Why don't you come to our house? We can talk over a cup of coffee, if that's okay with you." I have to admit this woman has my attention, and I'm curious why she needs to speak with me, of all people. Plus, I want to size her up on my own territory. People can be completely different creatures when not in their comfort zones.

I hastily give her the address and a suggested time, and disconnect. Marta's toast will be cold if I don't hurry, and I debate making more. Haste wins out, and I walk as quickly as I can, balancing both toast and tea without slopping the steaming drink over the sides of the mug.

Marta is sound asleep, lying on her side with one hand tucked under her cheek like a child, her lashes making dark crescents on her pale face. I carefully back out of the room, heading to the kitchen with the tray still in my hands. I'm tempted to see if I can carry it waiter style, balanced on one arm, but decide against it. I'd probably drop it and wake up Marta with the sound of crashing dishes.

I've already showered and dressed, so I flop down on the couch and thumb through my emails on my phone. Chrissy Burton will be arriving shortly, and I want to be distraction-free when she does. Something behind her words, something she didn't say on the phone, has me intrigued. Besides, I don't want to make any noise while Marta is getting some much needed rest.

But a look at my Google News feed sends me reeling. According to the *Alameda Dispatch*, a body was found early this morning, floating in the water just off the Oakland side of the Bay Bridge, identified as Chrissy Burton of San Leandro.

Unless Verizon has recently installed a cell tower in the great beyond, I could swear that's who I was just speaking with, the person I'm sitting here waiting for. I've made an appointment with a ghost.

CHAPTER TWO

C hrissy Burton arrives with fanfare, her car performing a noisy rendition of misfiring cylinders and spark plugs as she parks in front of my house. I peer out the front window in time to see a curtain twitch in the neighbor's window across the street, the self-proclaimed guardian of the 'hood. I tend to believe it's an aspiration for vicarious scandal that motivates old Mr. Flores rather than a true desire to keep the neighborhood safe. Marta tells me I'm too cynical and Mr. Flores is a "lovely man" who tells her the funniest jokes whenever they happen to meet.

Chrissy, with whom I've briefly spoken before at department holiday parties, disembarks from the mustard-colored Nova and checks her phone before heading to my door. She is a living, breathing cliché of the underpaid state worker or she's hanging on to a beloved car. Either one provides an interesting insight into the woman whose word is law at Alameda County Social Services. Folks who cling to the past tend to be high maintenance, just like the things they surround themselves with.

And folks who choose a career such as social work or teaching are either true saints or closeted martyrs. Marta is firmly ensconced in the first category, especially since she has to work with people such as Chrissy Burton. The clientele, she's assured me before, are the impetus behind everything she does. If she could do her job without the politics, she'd be in heaven. Conscious I have already prejudiced myself, I paste on a smile and open the door.

"Come in, come in," I say, forcing the words out between lips stretched wide in what must look like a parody of welcome. From the startled glance I get in return, Chrissy must agree with me. Something besides my deadhead's grin has her set on edge, but I guess there's nothing like hearing about your own death to start the day off on the wrong foot.

"Thanks for seeing me." She looks around the entry hall with hesitation as if trying to decide where to go next. "Is Marta all right?"

"She's sleeping right now, but it was a rough morning." I'm not sure if I want to discuss my partner's health with this woman, particularly after hearing her take on parenting.

I lead the way into our living room, its décor a modern take on Art Deco. Marta and I had both fallen in love with the remake of *The Great Gatsby*, and she had gone into a decorating frenzy, scouring estate sales and secondhand stores for facsimiles of the furnishings from the cottage where Nick Carraway, the story's narrator, had lived.

The walls are papered in an overlying stripe interior decorators of the '20s loved, and the furniture is solid walnut, upholstered in rich colors. A streamlined grandfather clock stands against the wall as if holding court, only its face telling how old it is. This is one of Marta's favorite finds, although it took me a while to get used to its persistent chiming. Now I scarcely hear it unless I'm in a hurry.

"This is gorgeous!" She halts in the doorway, and I can feel my bias softening just a bit. "Did you have an interior designer do this?"

"Sort of, and I'm sure she'd be flattered to hear you say that." I smile, gesturing to a carved sofa upholstered in muted gold and green. "Marta did it all. I'm just the muscle when it comes to things like this."

I rub my arms as if I can still feel the ache from all the tugging and moving I'd done until Marta had been completely satisfied with the placement of every piece of furniture.

"Please, have a seat. Can I get you anything, maybe coffee? Or tea?" I almost ask if she'd like a beer and think I might get one for myself. That unsettled vibe she's giving off is beginning to make me jittery as well.

"I'm not sure I should have any more caffeine." She gives a rueful laugh, running one hand over her face. I can see it trembling from across the room. "I must've drunk gallons of the stuff since I heard from the police department earlier."

Ah. Now we're getting down to business. I'll need a coffee, whether she does or not.

"Hold that thought." I stand up and head toward the kitchen. "I'm going to make coffee, but I'll grab a bottle of water for you, if you'd prefer."

"Yes, thanks." She stares out a window that looks out onto the side of the house. Marta has filled the narrow flower bed bordering the redwood fence with bulbs of every kind, mixing colors and types, ensuring something will always be blooming. I leave Chrissy contemplating the blossoms with a bemused expression on her face.

"Did I just hear you talking to someone?"

I jump sky high at Marta's voice. She's leaning against the granite-topped island, holding a bottle of water in one hand, the other resting across her stomach. I'm instantly at her side and put a steadying arm around her shoulders. She looks so pale and washed out next to the dark countertop.

"Hey, you need to be in bed, chica." I gently tug her toward the doorway, but she resists, craning her neck as she tries to look past me. "Want me to bring you some more toast?"

"You didn't answer my question, Gij. Who're you talking to?"

"Chrissy Burton."

"Wait. You're talking to my *boss*? Here? In our *house*?"

I nod, mouth twisted in a sheepish smile. Marta ducks beneath my arm and walks to the living room, a purposeful set to her slight shoulders. Sighing, I follow her. Apparently she's forgotten she's still dressed—or undressed—in the see-through nightie she put on after the latest visit to the bathroom.

"Chrissy! What's up?"

I skid to a halt just behind my partner, noting with amusement Chrissy is looking everywhere except at Marta and Marta is staring daggers at her boss. I don't blame her. I'd probably feel the same if Lou showed up unannounced, especially if I was feeling as poorly as Marta.

"How're you feeling, Marta?"

Chrissy directs the inquiry to a spot just behind my head. With a sigh, I back into the hall and grab a coat hanging in the hall closet. I place it on Marta's shoulders, and she draws it around herself as she moves toward an armchair that sits near the sofa. Chrissy finally allows herself to make eye contact with us, two pink spots on her cheeks a giveaway of her discomfort.

"I've been better." Marta's tone is as wry as her expression. "So, to what do we owe the honor?" She shoots me a glance as I sink down into the other chair. I pretend not to notice. Chrissy is on her own with this one.

Our guest silently looks down at her hands, clasped together on her lap, knuckles white and fingers tightly interwoven.

"I got a visit from the police early this morning, sometime

before five." She looks up, eyes bright with some emotion. I really am starting to need that coffee. "Apparently, the Alameda Sheriff's Department thought it was making a next-of-kin notification."

"'Apparently'?" Marta leans forward with interest, the flaps of the coat falling open slightly. Even from where I'm sitting I can see the prominence of her collarbones, emphasizing the weight loss she's had recently. "Why 'apparently,' Chrissy?"

"Because," Chrissy says in a matter-of-fact voice belied by her twisted fingers, "they were there to tell me I'd been found dead in the bay."

A woman has been discovered floating in the bay, something I already know because of my Google news feed. I also know the body was identified as Chrissy Burton, the gal now sitting across from me in my house. What I want to know is how the mix-up has occurred. Unless this is evidence of a stolen identity or someone who has—had—the same name as our guest, I can't figure out how something like this happens.

"And I'm assuming you set them straight, right?" Trust Marta to get to the heart of the issue.

Chrissy nods vigorously. "Yes." She gives a brief laugh that has no mirth in it. "Of course, it took me a few minutes to convince them. I had to show them my work ID, the key card with my picture attached. Even then I don't think that some of them believed me." Sudden tears appear in her eyes and begin running down her face. "And when they showed me a picture of the woman, I swear she looked just like me."

Marta walks over to the sofa, sitting down beside Chrissy and putting a thin arm around her.

"Whatever is going on, we'll help you figure it out. Won't we, Gij?" This last part is directed to me, her head tilted and one eyebrow raised in question. Marta in warrior woman mode. I nod, acquiescing to a higher power. When she has her mind set on a course of action, she will not be deterred. This is what makes her a force to be reckoned with as a social worker. Whatever case she has, she fights for the client with all of her heart.

Her very big heart. I recall her tenacious efforts last fall on behalf of my—*our*—nephew Leif. If it hadn't been for Marta's solid presence, I might have fallen victim to the circumstances as well.

"When Marta promises you we'll help, she means it." I stand up, hands on my hips. "Marta, would you like that tea now?" I smile down at her fondly. "You were sound asleep when I came up to the room earlier."

"Oh, please," Chrissy begins, half standing, her hands held out in front of her as if warding off an attack. And maybe she is. "Take care of Marta first. In fact," she adds as she checks her cell phone, "I probably should get going. I said I'd go down to the medical examiner's office so they could take a cheek swab to check my DNA. Guess I have to prove I'm really me." Marta cuts off Chrissy's short, mirthless laugh with a fierce hug.

"You're not going anywhere without us. Gij, I'll have that tea and toast now, and then I'll grab a shower." My partner is in full-blown caregiver mode, putting her own current frailty aside. Chrissy settles back down beside her, some of the anxiety disappearing from her face.

And I've gone into full-blown worrywart mode. I'm physically stronger than she is, but I don't know if I can carry an incapacitated Marta by myself. I'd hate for her to faint.

"If you think you're up to it," I say doubtfully.

I head to the kitchen and get out the bread, popping two more slices into the stainless steel toaster. While I wait for it to brown, I plug in the electric kettle, a throwback to my college days. I'd become fascinated with all things British, and having my own kettle made me feel a connection to a country I'd only read about or seen on television. Besides, it heated up water lightning fast, and I'd used it for making ramen soup more than I did to make tea.

I get out a seldom-used tray from the tall, narrow cabinet beside the fridge and place on it a small plate with plain toast and a mug of unsweetened hot tea. Marta's tastes have changed since she became pregnant, something the doctor assures us is completely normal. It's another reason I'm secretly glad she's the one carrying our child. I can't imagine giving up sweets or, even worse, not wanting them.

"Here you go," I say as I place the tray down on the low rectangular butler's table nestled close to Marta's end of the couch. Its fluted edges are elegant yet functional, ensuring nothing will be able to roll off. "Try to eat something, love."

❖

Marta says she feels better after her shower and the little bit of food she's managed to eat. Her color is better, thank goodness, but I know she's not up to driving. So I drive instead, with Chrissy in the front passenger's seat and the mama-to-be lying in the back seat.

The two women chat sporadically, mostly about work-related issues, while I concentrate on keeping my silver Honda CRV steady, not too fast, trying to time all the lights so I won't need to make a sudden stop. Their conversation gives me time to myself, and I can't help but recall the college writing class I'd taken and the professor who hated plot clichés with a passion.

"There are many reasons why falling back on a trope to move your story line is wrong, folks. The top of the list, though, is that it's just plain lazy writing." Mr. Harding had peered around the lecture hall from his perch on a tall stool, his back hunched and neck foreshortened inside the collar of his jacket.

I conjured up that memory because this entire situation has morphed into a trope of the highest degree: the unknown twin who commits some heinous crime and then allows an innocent look-alike to take the fall. How many Lifetime movies have revolved around that tired strategy? And how in the world did Marta and I get caught up in this?

I realize Marta has said something to me, and I drag my attention back to the present.

"Sorry, babe. I was miles away. What's up?"

"I was just saying," she begins, her words underpinned with some of her normal feistiness, "that you're driving this thing like my grandma. Chrissy wants to get this over with sometime in this decade, love."

I take a quick peek into the rearview mirror, pleased to see a sassy expression on her face. She's definitely feeling much better. I reach over and crank up the radio, ready to put the pedal to the metal. My favorite local station is playing "The Boys Are Back in Town." Perfect for Marta's return to the land of the living. With a grin, I send the CRV surging forward and leave the traffic snarled behind us.

The Alameda County Coroner's Office sits on a fairly quiet street in Oakland proper, its foundations sloping with the geography. I hit the parking jackpot, taking the only available space that just happens to be smack-dab in front of the walkway that leads to the coroner's office. Marta may be coming alive, but I'm still careful of how far she'll need to walk. I know better than to speak my concerns aloud, though. Marta hates being treated like a "cut glass figurine."

I tend to think of her as a Fabergé egg, holding a priceless treasure within herself that not even I can see. Yet. Marta's scheduled for an ultrasound in a few weeks, that miraculous scientific looking glass that will allow us to finally see the little person who'll be joining our family.

"I hope this swabbing test won't take too long." Chrissy pauses at the top of the ramp to wait for us, her eyebrows pinched together with growing stress. "And I hope it won't hurt." She gives a false laugh. "I never was that good with pain. Probably why I've never had kids of my own."

I just stare at her, trying to convey how clueless what she said is without saying a word. Marta wouldn't like that, I know. I'd like to give this woman some pain right now, though, right between her eyes.

Marta just smiles at Chrissy, one hand resting protectively on her belly and the other tucked beneath my arm. "It's not going to be a walk in the park, that's for sure. It's a good thing I've got Gij, otherwise I'd probably be scared shitless myself."

Well said, Marta. Well said. I almost follow that thought with a head toss but stop myself in time. There's enough tension here already without me adding to it. I realize Marta is poking me in the ribs while Chrissy gazes at me, one eyebrow lifted. I decide to play the poor hearing card.

"Sorry, guys. I totally missed what you said. Must be all the background noise." I gesture at the myriad eucalyptus trees framing the street, their branches filled with brash, noisy crows. A murder of crows. I shiver and feel Marta's hand tighten on my arm.

"I just asked you if you'd ever done any type of testing at your clinic." Chrissy pulls open the glass-fronted door and steps back so Marta and I can pass in front of her. "I was thinking it can't be much different, right? I mean, DNA is DNA."

"True," I agree as I guide Marta into the lobby of

the coroner's office. "And it should be something fairly noninvasive. Hair, for instance, or a cheek swab. Nothing too *painful*."

I can't help emphasizing that last word. Beside me I feel Marta sigh slightly. How she puts up with me I'll never know. With a bright smile, I turn to face Chrissy.

"There's the front desk. We'll wait for you over there." I point at a small grouping of chairs that look extremely uncomfortable, their molded plastic seats curved in that one-size-fits-all design. I think about the upholstered chairs and love seats in my clinic's waiting room and can't help feeling a bit smug. There's something to be said for a private enterprise versus taxpayer-funded offices.

They whisk Chrissy away through a light-colored wooden door and down a hallway that smells of antiseptic. I notice it faintly from where we're sitting, but Marta's olfactory senses are on overdrive. She wrinkles her nose and covers it with one hand.

"God, I thought these places were more modern now. What's with the morgue aroma?"

I shrug, my eye caught by a pile of magazines sitting neatly on a low scarred table. The editions are years out of date, of course, but the bold lettering on the top journal has me intrigued. "Are We Any Closer to Cloning Organs?" indeed.

Outside the window, I can see a cloud of black as the crows rise from the trees and fly off. A murder moving away from us, taking its shrill sounds to another part of the street. Try as I might, I have a feeling another murder has sucked us into its macabre vortex, courtesy of one Chrissy Burton.

Chapter Three

The ride back home is almost normal, a thin shield of casual conversation and observations covering the uneasiness each of us must feel. I know I do. I can't recall a more odd situation than the one in which I'm now involved.

Chrissy refuses Marta's invitation to come in for a coffee. I'm relieved. I've done my duty by this woman, and to be honest, I'm irritated Chrissy's problem has become Marta's. I'm almost gleeful as we stand outside watching the Nova pull away from the curb, its backfire an exclamation point to an unsettling few hours.

"Let's get you inside and resting, love." I guide her up the walkway into the house, giving Mr. Flores a cheeky wave with my free hand. He must be going bananas, watching the activity at my house without an inkling of what's happening. It almost raises my spirits.

"Surprisingly enough, I'm not feeling too bad right now." Marta sinks down onto the sofa, the cushions giving a small sigh of welcome as she settles back against the pillows. "In fact, considering I'm still off tomorrow and can sleep in, we could have a few friends in this evening. If you'd like to, of course," she adds hastily. "I know you probably have to go in to the clinic in the morning."

I kneel in front of the couch and put my arms gently around her, tempted to lay my head on her belly. I don't want to hurt her, though. If she's feeling as well as she says, I don't want to jinx it. Instead, I confine myself to a few brief kisses before standing up again.

"Sure, if you want to. We haven't seen Isobel and J.D. for a while. Or Maggie and Ann." The last time I can recall the six of us getting together was in the fall, just before I went to Arizona to deal with my sister's disappearance. Maybe it's time to dust off the ol' boogie shoes and let my hair down. "I can give them a holler, or maybe you can text them while I see what we've got in the fridge."

Marta smiles up at me. She *does* look much better in spite of the day's bad start and the morning's jaunt into Oakland. I can't resist kneeling back down and planting a tender kiss on her tummy. Marta places a hand on my head and gently runs her fingers through my hair, and my nearly dormant hormones stand to attention at her touch.

I'm just going in for a real kiss when the doorbell rings. Groaning, I drop my head for a moment before rising to my feet. "Hold that thought, love. I'll see who it is and get rid of them pronto."

I can see the top of Mr. Flores's head when I look through the peephole on the door. He is a small man, shrunken with age, and his sparse hair falls across his scalp like a baby's. Sighing, I open the door and look down at him with barely disguised irritation, ready to send to him packing.

"Good afternoon, Dr. C," he begins as he steps inside without an invitation. "Can I have a moment of your time, please?" His diminution of my name comes out as prissy rather than intimate.

"By all means," I say through clenched teeth, extending

an exaggerated flourish of welcome. "Marta's in the living room, if you want to go in there."

I follow him, giving Marta a look over his shoulders that says "not my fault" as he settles down in one of the armchairs, sitting on the edge with his back straight and his feet placed primly together. She barely stifles a grin before turning her attention to him.

"Mr. Flores, it's so good to see you. How've you been doing?"

He looks at me briefly as if to show me he's part of Marta's social circle before focusing on her face with an expression of concern.

"I'm doing well, thanks. And hopefully you're doing all right." He nods at the soft swell of her belly. "Are the babies letting you rest?"

I can't help it. I snort loudly as I slide onto the end of the sofa and lift Marta's feet onto my lap.

"She's not having twins," I say. "We don't have twins in our families." I glance over at her almost guiltily. She's the one doing all the work, after all. "At least Marta doesn't, and that's what counts."

"Hmm." It's not much of a response, but he's said a mouthful. He gives a slight shake of his head as if refocusing his thoughts before looking straight at me. "I came over to let you know you had a visitor after you left today."

"Really." The word comes out flat and cynical, elongated with sarcasm. But I'm not shocked. In fact, I suppose I've been expecting something like this ever since my first conversation with Marta's boss. Life has become a Tilt-A-Whirl, everything slightly askew. "Did you recognize him? Her?"

"Him. He is skinny, with hair like this." He uses one age-speckled hand to indicate a dramatic swoop of hair back from his face. I almost groan out loud.

"Sounds like Don Butler," I say to Marta. "And did he drive a Volkswagen van, white on top with faded gold paint on the bottom half?"

Mr. Flores nods vigorously. "Yes. And he parked it in front of a fire hydrant. I almost called the police." He leans back against the chair, arms folded high on his shrunken chest and mouth pursed in disapproval.

I chuckle despite my growing irritation. Mr. Flores, the keeper of the street. The guardian of our little galaxy. And full of useful information, as I discover.

"Well, thanks for letting us know." Marta smiles across at our visitor, shifting on the sofa so she faces him directly. "So, tell me what else is happening? How's your granddaughter? Any more news on her grades?"

I leave them chatting happily about various neighborhood doings and his granddaughter's latest academic accomplishment. I need to make a phone call.

I pause just long enough in the kitchen to brew a cup of coffee on my trusty Keurig before heading upstairs to our bedroom. I've left the bed unmade, so I feel absolutely no sense of guilt as I kick off my shoes and crawl under the chilly covers. I can talk to Don from here just as easily as from a chair.

There is history between me and the intrepid investigative reporter for the *San Leandro Times*. He made a name for himself a few years ago, uncovering a very illegal payday loan company's practice of adding hidden costs and raising the interest rate on a whim. His valiant actions helped thousands of unsuspecting borrowers recoup their money. However, when he stuck his twitchy nose into the drama that was my sister's disappearance, he lost his patina of heroism for me and became just another newshound looking for a good headline.

Still, the fact that he came to my house following the surprise visit from Chrissy Burton has my radar on high alert.

"*San Leandro Times*," says the cheery voice on the other end of the line, mercifully cutting short a tinny rendition of "Dust in the Wind."

"Don Butler, please." I don't explain the reason for my call. Thankfully, I'm not asked. I'm not sure I'd know how to define the reason anyway, given the odd set of circumstances I've already experienced.

I'm treated to the rest of the song while waiting for an answer. I finally hear a series of clicks and then Don's voice: "You've reached Don, and I'm either on another call or out saving the world. Leave a message after the tone."

Gag. His egotistical recording makes me think of Barry Dunwiddy, another reporter who thinks he's a gift to the modern world. He wormed his way into our lives for a short time when we were in Phoenix last fall until we managed to shake him.

I ask him to return my call, leaving my cell number. Disconnecting, I toss the cell phone onto the bed and fold my arms behind my head as I stare at the ceiling. From the hallway, I can hear Marta bidding Mr. Flores goodbye, then the thud of the front door shutting behind him.

"You can come out now, Gij. He's gone." Her voice is light, reminiscent of her pre-pregnancy self. Is it possible she's suddenly, miraculously past the worst of it?

"I'm not hiding," I begin to protest, but my words die off when Marta appears in the doorway to our room, a mischievous smile on her face and a sassy tilt to her hips. I'm on high alert, my addled hormones not far behind. I hold out one hand to her, and she falls onto the bed beside me, her face already lifted for my kiss.

My last coherent thought is that Don Butler and his ilk can go to hell.

To my amazement, we sleep through what remains of the day, stirring only briefly whenever we accidently brush against one another in the tangle of sheets. Marta is definitely acting like her old self, and I do my best to match emotion for emotion, touch for touch. It's as if she's on fire, determined to burn away every barrier, real or imagined. Trust me, I'm not complaining.

When the sun breaks through the curtains the next morning, I'm both sated and exhausted. Too much sleep, I think drowsily. Or too much Marta. The thought has me grinning before my eyes are even opened.

"What's so funny?"

I crack open one eye. Marta is standing on my side of the bed, her hair glistening as dark as a seal's, fresh from her shower. She's dressed, for goodness sake—dressed. And smiling.

"You're not going into work, are you?" I lift myself up on one elbow, using the other hand to flatten down my recalcitrant night hair. "I called you in yesterday. For today, I mean."

She nods in acknowledgment and sinks gracefully down on the bed, her weight tugging the covers from my shoulders. I wince as I struggle to sit up, my body sore from the night's lovemaking. Marta, on the other hand, looks positively radiant and well rested. Glowing, I think is the word most often used for women in her condition. I'm definitely *not* glowing.

She leans forward and plants a kiss on my forehead, her nose wrinkled in reaction to my "morning aroma," as we jokingly call it. Her sense of smell has been on high alert since the pregnancy, and I dive down under the covers, leaving only the top of my head and my eyes showing above the covers.

"Sorry," I mumble. I do not want to be the cause of a dash to the bathroom for a visit to the porcelain throne.

She laughs at me and jerks the covers down. "Don't be silly, silly. I was just kidding."

She stands back up, one hand resting lightly on her belly. From this angle, it's beginning to poke out at an alarming rate. Mr. Flores's sighting of the reporter the day before creeps back into my mind and I shove it away. I can only handle one issue at a time, and my attention is fully on my partner right now.

I toss back the comforter and get out of bed in one smooth motion, putting my arms around her, pulling her close. I rest my chin on top of her wet hair and take a deep breath, inhaling the invigorating scent of mint and eucalyptus.

"Feeling well enough to use the good stuff, huh?" Since the early stages of the pregnancy, Marta has barely been able to tolerate the unscented soaps and shampoo we had to buy to replace the highly scented washes we normally use.

"Yes, surprisingly enough." She leans back so she can look me in the eye. "I honestly feel fabulous today, Gij."

"That's good to hear, love," I say, giving her a gentle squeeze. She might be feeling great, but I'm still very conscious of the other person who's come between us, literally. When I hug her, I can feel the bump that means life as we know it is about to change.

"How about breakfast at the Vineyard?"

Her words take me aback for a second. It's been a while since we've visited any restaurant, fast food or otherwise. The Vineyard is one of our favorite places to go. Just thinking about their signature eggs Benedict makes my mouth water.

"I'd love to, if you think you're up to it." I move past her and head for the walk-in closet to choose clothes for the day. A shower is definitely in order, and I'm looking forward to using my own shampoo and body wash again. That unscented stuff just doesn't cut it.

"You have ten minutes," she says, and then she's gone, almost skipping down the stairs. I can hear her humming as she goes to the kitchen, a perky tune that fits the equally bright morning.

It's hard to imagine anything ruining this perfect day, but Don Butler's phone call comes just as we pull into the restaurant's parking lot, casting a slight pall over the sunshine. Not really, but it certainly feels that way.

Marta gives a small sigh and leans back against the padded headrest, her eyes closed behind her fashionably oversized sunglasses.

"Sorry, babe, gotta take this." I grimace apologetically at her as I answer the phone. "I'll make it quick."

"Dr. Cutler? This is Don Butler, *San Leandro Times*. I'm returning your call."

"And I was returning your visit," I say with mild amusement. One would think I'd been chasing the man. "One of my neighbors let me know you stopped by yesterday."

"Ah. Well, yes." I've stumped him. Maybe he's never come up against the likes of Mr. Flores before.

"What can I help you with? I'm just about to go into a meeting."

Marta's rotating her forefinger, telling me to wrap it up.

"Is there somewhere we can meet?" he says. "I've got a few questions for you, if you don't mind."

"I'll have to get back with you, if that's okay." We are polite, sidestepping any verbal mines that might explode, trapping us in a commitment.

"Not a prob. Hey, if it's all right, I'll call back in, what, two hours or so?"

"Sounds good. I look forward to your call," I lie, disconnecting. Marta's either heard both sides of the conversation, or she's developed a sixth sense. I'm inclined to think the latter.

"What's up with that?" She turns sideways with one hand on the armrest, ready to get out.

"Just a return call from that reporter. I left a message for him yesterday." I open my door and get out. "Stay there and I'll come around."

Marta snorts but does as I ask. We've never been one for ceremony, viewing ourselves as a pair of strong women who are quite capable of getting our own doors, thank you very much. Why I've suddenly reverted to this almost archaic behavior surprises both of us, but she smiles up at me as I take her hand and tuck it into my arm.

"Thanks for taking such good care of me, love."

"My pleasure," I reply, dropping a brief kiss on her forehead.

The Vineyard is busy but not unpleasantly so, the tables and booths occupied with young professionals and retirees. The hum of voices is muted, and the acoustic music that plays in the background has never been overpowering. Thank goodness. Whether I like to admit it or not, the older I get, the more I tend to dislike music that causes conversations to be conducted at near-screaming levels.

It can make a real scream hard to hear. When one reverberates from the parking lot and startles the entire restaurant, I drop Marta's hand and race back outside. From where I stop just beyond the front door, I see a woman lying on the asphalt, a distraught man kneeling by her side.

CHAPTER FOUR

The Vineyard is far from staid, but it has seen nothing like this before. The restaurant's staff and clientele have spilled out on the sidewalk into the carefully manicured shrubbery, staring at the confusion in the parking lot. From where Marta and I are standing, arms around one another, I can see the man who was kneeling at the woman's side. His hair is flying wildly about his thin, sun-darkened face, but the way he stands seems familiar to me, the way his uses his hands to tell a story. Maybe he's a client at the vet clinic.

Making sure Marta has a place to sit apart from the gawping crowd, I push forward and approach one of the officers standing at the scene's periphery. She is rapidly tapping a note or a text into an oversized smartphone and only looks up when I move in front of her and stop.

"Can I help you?" She tucks the cell phone back into a front uniform pocket and waits for my response, thumbs hooked loosely into her wide leather belt.

I have to tilt my head up in order to look directly into eyes so green their color must be courtesy of contacts and not DNA. Either way, I have to admit they're rather nice to look at, compelling even. Focus, I warn myself.

"My name is Dr. Giselle Cutler, and I'm the one who

called this in to 9-1-1." I look over my shoulder toward the controlled chaos around the woman's body and then back at the officer, who stares down at me impassively. "I'm involved marginally in the Chrissy Burton case and just wondered if this might have something to do with it."

"I see." The two words are mild, yet they send a wave of heat up my neck and into my face. I sound like a total idiot.

"Can I ask how you're involved, Doctor? Marginally, that is." She makes the request in a respectful tone, but I still flush. She's probably already marked me down as someone who watches *CSI*. I do, but that's beside the point.

The allure of those green eyes is beginning to fade ever so slightly. I've never been a fan of someone who passively jeers at others, particularly when the taunting is aimed in my direction. I straighten my shoulders and stare back at her. I feel as though I've been summed up and found wanting. Or guilty.

"My partner, Marta Perry, is a social worker for Alameda County." Officer Green Eyes nods ever so slightly. Good. At least she's following me. "Her direct supervisor, Chrissy Burton, was supposedly found dead in the bay yesterday morning. Actually, it was someone who has the same name and who looks like her, but it's not Chrissy." I'm not making much sense but it's as clear as I can get under such scrutiny. "The real Chrissy Burton came to our house yesterday."

She unhooks the radio from her belt. "Sarge, I've got the caller here, says she may know something about the vic."

I just stare at her, too aghast to protest. I've said nothing of the sort. Has the woman not heard a single word I've said?

"Everything all right here?"

I turn to see Marta standing behind me, and I breathe a sigh of relief. She'll know how to handle this. Her floaty top and delicate features give her a frail, ethereal appearance. She is far from either, though. I almost want to sell tickets to what I'm sure will become a showdown worthy of an audience.

"Officer, this is my partner, Marta Perry." Marta nods graciously, silently, and slips one hand though my arm. Her presence is more than comforting. It's strength giving, empowering. I decide to take on the law myself, and I incline my head at the officer. "She thinks I know something about the victim, the woman who was hit."

To my amazement, Marta twists her mouth into a grimace. It telegraphs irony and sadness as brightly as any neon sign.

"You might not know her, love, but I thought I recognized her. *If* it's who I think it is, her name is Beverly Strait, and she's Chrissy's PA." She turns to the officer, who has begun tapping the phone's screen furiously. "Is she going to be all right?"

Before the officer can answer, I break in.

"Wait a sec. You mean she works with you?" My brain is starting that Tilt-A-Whirl thing again, common sense slamming against incredulity with an almost gravitational force that dizzies me. "What's going on here, Marta?"

She shrugs, a troubled expression on her face. "Your guess is as good as mine, Gij. That's why we let the police deal with things like this, right?" She squeezes my arm softly. That's her signal to move back, to separate ourselves from the action in the Vineyard's parking lot. The gurgle in my stomach convinces me to listen. "Besides, if it really is Bev, someone will need to call Chrissy."

"If there's nothing else, Officer, I need to get Marta in front of some food. Gotta keep the little one happy." I reach over and give Marta's belly a pat.

Only the slightest lift of one eyebrow gives away any

reaction. "Just need your full name and a good number to reach you, if necessary."

To my amazement, this comment is directed to Marta, not me. After a quick information share and a promise to call the police department if she can think of anything that might be helpful, Marta tugs me back toward the restaurant. We make the brief walk in silence, and I can clearly hear the commotion that still surrounds the victim. I shiver suddenly, and Marta tightens her hand on my arm.

"You okay, Gij?"

"Yeah, I'm fine." I lean over and deposit a quick kiss on her forehead. "I don't know about you, babe, but I'm starving." I keep my voice light, attempting to dispel the gloomy cloud that has settled over the morning "I could eat a horse."

"Oh, gag." Marta feigns disgust, pulling her hand away as she opens the door. "You can have the horse. I want a veggie omelet." She grins at the hostess, who is listening avidly to our exchange. "I'd like to sit in the non-horse section, please."

I shake my head as we follow the giggling hostess to a table in front of the window, clearly prime real estate, a place to see and be seen. Fabulous. A front-row seat to the drama going on in the parking lot.

Marta, attentive as always to my feelings, asks for a table farther back. I smile at her gratefully. The hostess flicks her ponytail, clearly put out. Some people, her eloquent back seems to say, just don't appreciate the finer things in life.

We settle in our chairs, and I'm amused when I see the man sitting across from us take more than a passing glance at Marta. She's lovely in a fine china sort of way, her skin almost translucent in the slanting sunshine. Unable to resist the devil on my shoulder, I lean over and gently place one hand on her cheek. There. Territory established. From the corner of my eye, I see him give a minute shake of his head and dive back into his newspaper.

"Should I text Chrissy, or do you think it's better to call her?"

I have to mentally shake my own head and focus my attention on Marta's words.

"That's totally up to you, love." I reach out and straighten the silverware lying in front of me, imagining they're surgical instruments in my clinic. On second thought, no. I've seen shinier utensils in my own kitchen.

"Maybe I'll just send a text right now, if you don't mind." She's already reaching in her soft leather bag for her cell phone, belying the courtesy of her words. That's Marta for you, though. She decides on a plan of action and makes you think it was your idea all along. Clever.

A wiry young man with a wispy ponytail and an even wispier goatee arrives, bearing menus and iced water. With a promise he'll return shortly for our orders, he almost pirouettes as he turns to the next table. I want to giggle. He's either a frustrated ballet dancer or an overgrown child, unable to walk when twirling will do.

"Okay, that's done." Marta puts the phone on the table next to her and smiles across at me. "Any idea what you're going to get? And don't give me that line about a horse again."

"The usual," I say, tossing the menu aside, narrowly missing my water glass. "And I think I want an order of their breakfast bruschetta as well. Want to split one with me?"

The Vineyard's signature breakfast bruschetta is an amazing combination of gouda and Swiss cheeses along with thickly sliced bacon. It's layered on freshly baked Italian bread brushed with olive oil, then broiled until the cheese is golden brown and the bacon is sizzling. By the time it arrives at our table, I'm beginning to regret the invitation to share it. In typical Marta fashion, she cuts it in two, pushing the smaller piece toward me. I just manage to control a scowl.

"I'm eating for two," she says by way of an explanation as she takes a bite of the bread, her eyes bright with mischief. "Unless you want this back, of course." She brandishes her piece of the bruschetta at me. I'm not fooled by her act of contrition. It's just her way of saying there's no way on God's green earth I'm getting it out of her hand. The rest of the food arrives and soon we are deep into eggs and conversation, discussing Marta's idea for the room we've dubbed "the nursery." She wants to use gender-specific colors, which amuses me. I'm all for slapping up a few decals on the walls and calling it done.

"You have no sense of design," she says with a sniff. "And we'll have to wait, anyway. I want to get the ultrasound done first so we can see what we're having. For the color scheme."

"For the color scheme," I agree, my tone just this side of sarcastic. She gives me a sharp glance and goes back to cleaning her plate, something I haven't seen her do in what feels like years.

Just as the waiter twirls back with the check, Marta's phone begins to vibrate. She checks the screen, and I can see her eyes narrow slightly as she scans the message. She's either not happy with what it says, or she needs the reading glasses she's probably left at home.

"What's up?" I reach for the check and glance at it before adding my bank card to the small tray. Two chocolate truffles are lying there as well, maybe to soften the blow of the cost. I take one and toss the other in Marta's direction. She ignores it, continuing to stare at her phone with a frown on her face.

"Chrissy says someone already called her about Bev.

Apparently she's fine, just bruises and bumps from walking into a moving car." Marta looks up at me, and I can tell she's not buying Chrissy's explanation. I'm not either. Who in their right mind walks into a car, especially when it's moving?

"Does she say why Bev was here in the first place?"

Marta glances back down at the phone and shakes her head.

"No, so I'm assuming she was here to eat, same as us." She pauses a moment. "It's kind of odd, though. Both Chrissy and Bev out on the same day, I mean."

"Not really," I say as I hand the tray to the hovering waiter. "Bev's boss is dealing with something pretty weird right now, so she's probably taking advantage of Chrissy being gone. You know, a mental health day."

"Not if you know Beverly Strait the way I do." Marta's voice is firm. "That woman lives for running the office, and she'd have full run of the place with Chrissy out of the way." She shakes her head slowly. "No, I think there's something else going on besides that body in the bay. Or maybe because of it."

"I thought I recognized the man she was with," I say abruptly.

"Really? As in someone you know or maybe someone from work?" Marta smiles up at the waiter, who's returned with the slip for me to sign. "Thanks."

"Yeah," he says, but he clearly has something else to add.

"Is there anything else?" I know I sound a trifle snappish, but I don't like wait staff that hovers.

"Yeah," he says again. "I know that guy out there, the one with the woman who got run over."

I start to correct him, but Marta jumps in.

"Is he a friend of yours?"

He shrugs. "Sorta. That's my brother."

Marta and I just stare at him, neither one of us knowing what to say to this new revelation. Can the day get any stranger?

"He was just dropping off some money he owes me." The waiter, who I now see is called "Jinx" according to the name badge clipped to his polo's collar, smiles broadly, showing a set of impressive straight, white teeth. "And I was gonna find out how I can get in on the gig as well."

"The gig?" I repeat, glancing briefly at Marta. "Is he in a band?"

He laughs, a surprisingly deep, husky sound. A few diners swivel around to stare at us, and I pat the table in front of an empty chair.

"Can you sit for a minute?"

"Sure," he says as he slips gracefully into the seat. "I'm actually off shift. I just need to turn in your receipt." He nods toward the curled slip of paper still in front of me.

"So, tell us about this gig." I'm asking instinctively, not because I'm a people person, but because this entire past twenty-four hours have been something out of Lewis Carroll's imagination. I figure one more odd conversation won't hurt.

"Well, I'm not sure of the details, which is why I wanted to talk to him about it, but it's something to do with transplants."

"With *transplants*, did you say?" I'm now convinced I have indeed fallen down a rabbit hole. "What sort of transplants?"

"That part I'm not too sure about. I think, and don't quote me, it has something to do with bones." He gives a small shake of his head, his forehead furrowed. "I didn't know you could transplant bones, you know?"

"Bone marrow." My mind is racing around, trying to gather up the loose ends of my thoughts and tie them into some semblance of logic. "Did your brother donate bone marrow?"

Jinx shakes his head emphatically. "Nah, not him. He

doesn't donate anything. Like I said, he owes me money, so I figured this is from the transplant gig." I'm still staring at him, my eyes wide and my mouth slightly open. "He got paid for his donation thingy. That's what I mean." Jinx sounds like he's trying to explain something to a child. A not so very bright child. I snap my mouth shut.

Marta, who has been listening silently to this exchange, pats Jinx on the arm. "Thank you for taking time to explain things to us. Would you mind if I got your number? Just in case we have more questions."

Jinx nods. "Sure. It's…" and he rattles off his number so quickly I barely have time to fish out my cell phone. Marta, thank goodness, has managed to capture it and repeats it back to him.

"I'll text you right now so you'll have my number as well." Her fingers fly across the screen, and Jinx's phone pings from his apron pocket. "There. And my name is Marta."

"I'm Giselle."

"I know." Jinx grins down at me as he stands. "It's on your tab."

With a twirl and a smile, he reaches for the signed credit card slip and is gone.

I look across at Marta. "I'm not sure I like the idea of someone knowing my name like that."

This time it's her turn to shake her head at me.

CHAPTER FIVE

The parking lot has cleared out of rescue vehicles by the time we exit the Vineyard, but a few crime scene techs are still measuring and taking pictures. Officer Green Eyes is now sitting in the front seat of her cruiser, speaking into a hand-held radio and smoking. Judging by the way she's holding the cigarette out the window, it's probably frowned on by the department.

I look down at Marta and put my arm around her ever-expanding waist, very glad she doesn't smoke. I once dated a girl in college who did a great impression of a chimney, and her kisses tasted like an ashtray. Marta, I'm glad to say, does not taste that way at all.

"What?" She's looking up at me, one eyebrow quirked.

"*What* what?" I smile at her, giving her a little squeeze. She's caught me staring at her and we both know it, but I like pretending I have no idea what she's talking about. "Ready to get out of here?"

"Yes," she says, but the word's inflection means exactly the opposite.

"Okay, you. What're you thinking?"

I open the Honda's passenger door for her, making sure

she's settled before I shut it and walk around to the driver's side. I slip the keys into the ignition but don't start the engine, facing Marta instead.

"Doesn't it seem odd that we decide to go out for breakfast and run into all this?" She gestures to the parking lot, a serious expression on her face. "Of all the places to choose, we come here."

"Of all the gin joints in all the towns in all the world…" I say, doing my best Bogey imitation and brandishing a pretend cigar. She shushes me with a wave of her hand.

"I'm serious, Gij. Don't you think it's the universe trying to push us into something?"

My automatic reaction is to joke, but Marta is very solemn in her pronouncement, staring over at me with an expectant air. Dear Lord. Has the woman started studying Gaianism behind my back?

"I don't know about the universe."

"Okay, maybe not the universe." She gives a half-smile of acknowledgment. "But something is definitely putting this together, Gij. I think we need to pay attention."

She has a point. I'm just not sure what it is.

Out of my periphery, I can see one of the techs beginning to wind up the yellow crime scene tape, calling out to someone else and laughing as she does. Another day, another scene. Not the restaurant's best foot forward. Not Beverly Strait's, either.

"It's certainly one big coincidence, love. Other than that, I don't know." I give her thigh a pat and turn the key in the ignition. "Would it make you feel better to give Chrissy a call and tell her about Jinx and his brother?"

Her smile is a brilliant and sharp as the sun. "I already planned on it."

Of course she did. She wouldn't be Marta if she hadn't.

If anyone dislikes leaving the proverbial stone unturned, it would be my partner.

"Well, no time like the present." I back out of the parking spot and purposely head to an exit on the other side of the lot, skirting what's left of the scene. "Besides, I want to hear what she's got to say."

By the time we are out on the road, Marta has her boss on the phone.

"Hey, it's Marta." I can barely hear the muffled response. I point to my ear and Marta shakes her head but asks anyway. "Can I put you on speaker, Chrissy? Giselle is here as well." When I can finally hear Chrissy's voice and we've exchanged greetings, Marta jumps right in. "Do you know someone named Jinx?"

"Jinx? I don't think so. Why?"

"Or does Bev?" I say.

"I'm not sure. What's this all about, Marta?"

Marta gives a brief report as I listen, ready to jump in if needed. She covers it all, though, and I'm left eavesdropping on the back and forth between her and her boss. She pauses at the end of her recitation.

The silence on the other end of the line is deafening. I give her space to process. After all, this is a woman who was declared dead only yesterday. Coming back into the land of the living can be a treacherous endeavor.

"Can I invite myself over again?" The abrupt question clearly startles Marta but I nod, forgetting Chrissy can't see my response.

"Absolutely," Marta says, recovering quickly. "When would be good for you?"

"I'd like to stop by as soon as possible. If that's okay," she adds hastily. "Giselle, would that be all right with you? I know you've taken today off to be with Marta."

"No worries," I assure her. "I have a feeling we'll both be back at work on Monday, so today might be the last time we have off together for a while."

"Except when the baby gets here." Marta jabs me in the side, and I wince. She's got strength behind that poke. She's already taking on the role of mama bear, protecting her cub from even imagined slights. The thought makes me wince mentally. I need to get on board.

"Yes, ma'am. Except when the baby gets here." I make my voice quasi-contrite and Chrissy laughs, her disembodied merriment bouncing around the inside of the CRV. Marta gives me a sassy look, tossing her head.

We make it to the house and have enough time to pick up a few scattered items and plump the living room pillows before Chrissy Burton arrives in her vintage Nova. As in her previous visit, it announces her presence via a series of backfires, a modern-day herald trumpeting her arrival. I imagine Mr. Flores flicking his curtains aside to better see the action in front of my house.

"Don't knock it," I say as I head to the front door. "No car payment is a good thing."

"I suppose," Marta calls from the kitchen. She's decided to put the French press to use instead of making individual cups of coffee with the Keurig. "Should I open a bag of cookies or something?"

"It's up to you, love. You know me. I could eat sugar any time." I see Chrissy's outline through the wavy glass inset on the side of the front door and pull it open before she has a chance to ring the bell. "Welcome back," I say, trying for a hearty tone. "Marta's just putting the coffee on."

We settle ourselves in the living room much as we did yesterday: Marta reclining on the couch with her feet on my lap, and Chrissy ensconced in the armchair nearest the window. I take a sip of my coffee and set it down, ready to learn whatever I can about Bev Strait and her involvement with Jinx's brother.

"First of all, what's the latest on Bev?" Marta typically starts conversations by asking about someone else's health. "Any word on how long she'll be in the hospital?"

"It's not as bad as it looked." Chrissy takes a tentative sip of coffee before reaching for the plate of soft-baked cookies Marta has placed nearby. "Outside of minor scrapes and bruises, the worst injury she has is a concussion, where her head hit the pavement. They say she'll be just fine."

"That's good news," I say. Both women look at me as if I've sprouted horns. "Well, it's better than being, you know, dead. Right?"

"Straight to the point as always," Marta says, but she takes the sting out of her words with her smile. "And yes, it's definitely better than being dead. Speaking of which, is there anything else on that woman they found in the bay?" she asks Chrissy.

Our guest shakes her head. "Nothing yet. We're waiting for the results of that DNA test." She glances down at her feet for a moment, her bottom lip caught in her teeth. She's clearly debating with herself. Or she has more information than she's intimated, and she's trying to backpedal.

"What is it?" Marta's voice is soft and gentle, coaxing but not pushy.

"It's the test." Chrissy looks up and I'm curious to see that her eyes have filled with tears. "It's not going to help, to be perfectly honest."

Marta and I exchange a brief glance. Why wouldn't a DNA test help? It could show the dead woman is either related or she's not, plain and simple. And even if that's the case, Chrissy's family wouldn't be the first to have skeletons in their closet. How many adults have gone through their late parents' things only to find out that they were adopted? It's certainly within the realm of probability if not possibility.

"Would you like to tell us about it?" Marta asks. "If not, that's okay. But we're here for you whenever you need to talk."

Chrissy wipes at her streaming eyes with the backs of her hands. Taking in a deep breath that seems more like a shudder, she says, "It's because of two things. First of all, I had a bone marrow transplant when I was eight. Childhood leukemia."

"Chrissy! I had absolutely no idea." Marta leans forward, and I'm irrationally scared she'll smash the baby. "And how are you doing now, healthwise?"

Chrissy shrugs. "I'm fine. I was one of the lucky ones. We caught it early, and we had access to great medical care. To tell you the truth, I can hardly remember anything about the transplant itself."

The three of us sit in silence for a few minutes. Chrissy's revelation is another reminder of how little we know about the people we work with on a daily basis. It makes me wonder what I don't know about Lou.

"You said there's something else." Marta's voice invites confidences.

"Well, it's not as earthshaking as leukemia." Chrissy gives a short laugh that sounds dangerously close to a sob. "I'm adopted."

"That won't affect a DNA test," I say, ignoring the look Marta shoots in my direction. "If anything, it can help us see just how successful the transplant was." When both women just stare at me without comment, I add, "A person's DNA makeup is completely changed by a bone marrow transplant. The recipient takes on the markers of the donor, overriding the original DNA."

Chrissy nods in agreement. "True, and I'd already thought of that, to be honest. I really don't have any way to show the identity of my birth parents and who might be a relative or not. I mean, I have no idea how many children my birth mother had."

"Wouldn't the agency have a record of who gave you up for adoption? Most reputable agencies keep fairly complete records. You'd need a court order to get at them, of course, but they should be there." Marta looks from Chrissy to me. I nod.

"There's still the weird thing about her name," I remind them. "What're the odds that both of you, especially if you turn out to be related, would have the exact same name?" I look at Chrissy, more to register her response than anything else.

"How did the officers identify her? Did they tell you? Or show you her ID?"

Judging by the expression on Chrissy's face, Marta has just hit on an aspect that she's not thought about.

"I have no idea," she says. "Do you think we should ask about that?"

I notice the use of an inclusive pronoun. Has this become a "we" situation without me being aware of it?

Marta reacts emphatically. "Absolutely. If I were you, I'd wonder about the type of identification they had on her. Was it a driver's license? An insurance ID card?" She looks at me for confirmation. I lift my chin at her, wordlessly telling her to continue. "They obviously had something that made them think they had a deceased woman named Chrissy Burton."

"Who just happened to be living at the same address as the live woman," I say, thinking aloud. "Why didn't this occur to us sooner? It's obvious, now that we're talking about it."

"What's obvious?" Marta sounds a bit snappish, a sure sign she's beginning to tire. I ignore her, concentrating on my current train of thought.

"No, seriously. Think about it. What're the odds she'd

share your name *and* your address? About zero to a zillion. I think she was carrying something of yours, Chrissy. Something with a picture. That alone would make them sure they'd gotten the right identification."

"Especially if she looked something like me." Chrissy sits up straighter, dried tears still on her face. "Do you think I should call the officer who came to my house?"

"Without a doubt. And the sooner the better. I think she needs to be ID'd, and then we can decide what to do."

"Gij, if you don't mind me saying so, I think we've missed another link in the chain."

Marta's demeanor is calm, her voice still serene, but I can see the beginnings of dark smudges under her eyes. She's overdone it.

"Is this something that can wait?" I lean over and take her hands in mine. "You're looking kinda tired, love."

"It can probably wait, but I want to tell you before I forget. Pregnancy brain," she says with a laugh, touching the side of her head. "I feel like I'm losing my mind some days. Gij, remember what Jinx told us about his brother and the bone marrow donation? I know it's a tenuous link, but with Chrissy being a transplant recipient and Bev hanging out with someone who's obviously selling his bone marrow, I can't help thinking there has to be a connection somewhere."

I shake my head in confusion, trying to follow her convoluted reasoning. "I think we should talk about this tomorrow," I say, inching out from under her feet and standing up. "And Chrissy needs to call to find out about the identification. Sorry to cut this short," I say to Chrissy. "Marta needs to get in bed and rest, and I want to make a few notes about the things we've learned and heard. And seen," I add, thinking about Bev and the accident at the Vineyard.

"I'll go lie down," Marta says, "but I want your promise

you'll come and tell me right away if you think of anything important. Scout's honor?"

I laugh and extend a pinkie. "Even better, love. Let's pinkie swear."

Judging by the expression on her face, Chrissy must think we're half crazy. I beg to differ. Life with Marta is either all or nothing. And I happen to love living this crazy life with her.

Chapter Six

With Chrissy gone and Marta tucked up in bed, I pour myself a glass of Cabernet and stretch out on the sofa, extending my legs and resting my back against its gracefully curled arm. I can even see Marta's touch there. She'd insisted on extra padding, pooh-poohing the threat of a "lumpy presentation" by the snooty upholsterer. The look of chagrin on the man's face when the sofa was delivered was payment enough for my sassy partner. She'd been right. As usual.

I dug out a spiral notebook from under a stack of baby magazines Marta has collected at every doctor's visit. It's partially filled with ideas for baby names, color choices for the room we've designated as the nursery, and lines from poems and songs she wants to stencil on the walls. Careful not to disturb Marta's writing, I turn to the back of the notebook and begin my own list.

First, there is the dead woman herself. How did she end up in the bay? Suicide? I make a note, adding a series of question marks after the words. Of course, it could also be an accident. Or murder. I add both.

And then there's her name. Of course, this woman might truly have the name Chrissy Burton. Marta's boss does not have a monopoly on it. I'm sure other Giselle Cutlers are out there as well. It's hard to believe there is another Marta Perry, though. She's one of a kind.

The address is the stumper. I can't explain how or why the officers would even have the exact address at which the live Chrissy resides. I'm not an expert on law enforcement, but they had to have gotten the address from a source they felt certain about. Otherwise, I can only imagine the mix-ups that might occur, the incorrect death notices given. More question marks, underlined.

And then there's the entire sideshow with Bev and Jinx's brother. I'm not sure what else to call it. I'm still processing the series of coincidences that have happened up to this point. I sit for a few minutes, pen hanging loosely from my fingers as I go back over the past thirty-six hours. It almost makes Marta's suggestion of the universe's intervention seem sensible.

When my cell phone begins to sing, I start from my reverie.

"Giselle Cutler," I say, fully expecting to hear Lou's voice on the other end.

"It's Don, *San Leandro Times*."

Crap. I've completely forgotten his promise to call me back.

"Sorry I couldn't talk earlier, Don. I've been a little preoccupied." Here's a resource that might help me, right at my fingertips. Taking in a deep breath, I say, "Are you available to meet?"

"Sure." His prompt response gives me pause, but only for a second. He's probably viewing me as a resource as well. "Just give me the when and where, and I'll be there."

I hesitate inviting him to the house, but he's already been here. In for a penny, in for a pound.

"How far away are you from my house?"

"Just down the block." I shouldn't be surprised.

"Well, come on over. I'll get the coffee going."

Don Butler is as slight and wiry as I remember, built like a terrier with a nose for news. His eyes meet mine with a ferocity that belies his size, and I can imagine him playing David to society's Goliath without any problem. He'll tackle any topic, any time, no worries.

"Nice digs." He pauses in the doorway to the kitchen and looks around, taking in the stainless steel and granite splendor. I am inordinately proud of it, considering it's not even my comfort zone.

"Cream and sugar?" I carry two full mugs to the table in an alcove overlooking the front yard.

"Just black," he says, reaching for one of the mugs and taking a tentative sip. "Ah, that's good stuff." He grins up at me, his face transformed into that of a mischievous boy who's managed to find the hidden cookies. "You can't imagine the shit that passes for coffee at the newspaper."

"Trust me, I can," I say as I drop into a chair opposite him. "Marta's office has the most God-awful brew. She refuses to drink it, says it'll eat the lining out of any self-respecting stomach." She's got her own Keurig sitting in her cubicle, making her the most popular girl on the playground right around two o'clock every afternoon.

We sip in silence for a moment, and I strain to hear any sound from upstairs. Marta needs her rest today, especially if she's going back to work on Monday. Finally, Don puts his mug down and stretches his legs, his knees popping with a sharp crack.

"If that doesn't tell you how old I am,…" He grimaces, reaching down to rub at the offending joints. "When I think of how many miles I must have walked just to get a story."

"Kinda makes the pet care business seem tame." Of course, I face other issues like nips from frightened dogs or a face full of claws when a cat doesn't want to cooperate. "I'm guessing you're not here to discuss the perils of the working world, though."

"True." He stares directly at me, and I can only imagine being on the interviewee's hot seat. "So, tell me what you know about the kerfuffle with Chrissy Burton."

"As you probably already know, Chrissy Burton, an office supervisor at Alameda County Social Services, is alive and well. Unfortunately, she shares a name with the dead woman."

"As well as an address? Come on, Dr. Cutler. Doesn't that seem a tad far-fetched to you?"

"Absolutely," I say, leaning forward, my voice earnest. "And that's why you're the perfect person to help me figure out exactly what's going on."

His expression is almost comic: eyes opened as wide as they'll go, mouth agape, neck jutting forward like a bantam rooster defending his territory. I have to push the visual aside so I don't laugh.

"Are you serious or just pullin' my chain?" He leans back and folds his arms across his chest, a mute display of protection. So much for the legendary newsman who lives to ferret out a juicy story.

"Oh, she's serious."

We both turn to see Marta leaning against the doorway with a grin on her face. She's remembered to pull a robe over her sleepwear this time. Still, her ability to materialize silently makes me think she's developed a new talent along with the pregnancy. It'll come in handy when we have a teenager in the house, but for now it's rather disconcerting.

"Are you sure you should be out of bed?" I have to consciously keep the querulous tone tamped down, not wanting to sound like a spoiled child whose plans have been disrupted. I'm just worried about her health, making me appear snappish.

"I'm fine," she says, coming around the table to drop a kiss on my head before sitting down. "Is there any more of that?" She looks pointedly at my coffee mug.

"I take it congratulations are in order." Don raises his coffee in a salute. "I never had the privilege myself, so I admire those who do."

"You'd have been in the *Guinness Book of World Records* if you had," I can't resist saying as I make a cup of decaf. His laughter eases the remaining tension from the room. Marta just shakes her head at my bad joke as I hand her a brimming mug and plant my own kiss on her tousled hair.

"Is this a private counsel of war, or can anyone join?" Marta watches me over the rim of her coffee mug.

"Anyone can join, but first you need to be sworn to secrecy." I draw my forefinger across my throat. "What's said at the table stays at this table. Unless, of course, we need to tell the police."

"Speaking of, has your boss heard anything else from them concerning the woman's true identity?" Don says. He watches Marta, his face expressionless. He's baiting the trap, I think, and then wonder where that thought came from. He's either here to help, or he's out on his butt.

"Well, we went with her to do a DNA test yesterday." Marta offers after a brief glance in my direction. "She doesn't think it will do any good, though."

I instantly know where she's going with that last comment. "Marta, I don't think it's ours to tell." And I'm not sure it's a good idea to tell a journalist about Chrissy's private history.

"At this point, she needs all the help she can get, and her story is part of it, don't you think?"

I hesitate before lifting one shoulder in a small shrug. "I guess. You know her better than I do."

"That I do." Marta looks directly at Don, squaring her

shoulders as though facing a challenge. "Chrissy told us a couple of things about herself that might have something to do with the ID mix-up. First of all, she was adopted as a baby and has no idea about her birth mother, how many siblings she might have, nothing."

Don reaches for his pocket and then hesitates. "Is it okay if I record this conversation?"

"No," Marta and I say in concert, our voices raised.

"All right, all right." Don raises his hands in mock surrender. "Don't jump down my throat and stomp on my liver."

"Well, that's a new one," I say. "From the South, are we?"

Don grins, emphasizing the lines at the corners of his eyes. "I'm what you might call a first-generation Yankee. My entire family is from either Louisiana or Mississippi, and I grew up in a typical Southern home, only it was here in California."

"Back to Chrissy." Once Marta's focused, she isn't a fan of tangents. "She also had health issues when she about seven or eight, which led to a bone marrow transplant. So, according to the good doctor here," she says with a wink in my direction, "her DNA won't be what she was born with."

"It's because the—" Marta waves away the rest of my commentary.

"We get it, we get it, love. And I'm sure Don knows about things like that as well. Right?" This last question is aimed at our guest, who nods. "See?"

"Whatever," I mutter as I take a sip from my cooling coffee. "See if I help you with your science homework anymore." Marta sticks out her tongue.

Judging by the raised eyebrows on Don's face, he must think we're crazy. We are. It helps keep us balanced.

"I think we need to begin at the beginning," Don says. He leans forward, hands clasped in front of him on the table.

"From where I stand, I see two pathways we need to go down—your boss's birth family and how in the hell the police thought the dead gal lived with your boss."

Brilliant. I'd already figured that one out on my own. I have to remind myself he has much better resources than I do, though. It wouldn't do to isolate him at this point.

"Can you do some digging and find out who her parents were? Or at least her mom?" Marta's face is anxious. I know she might be at loggerheads with Chrissy at work, but she doesn't want to see anyone get hurt.

"Piece of cake." Don sounds confident, leaving me wondering just how private our private lives are. Still, it's a necessary evil at this point, if only to help Chrissy Burton figure out if she has any connection to the dead woman.

"If you do that, Giselle and I can make a few phone calls today and see if we can figure out how the whole address thing happened." Marta, I can see, has gone into planner mode.

"I'm pretty sure we don't have the authority to do that, love." I'm playing the role of wet blanket today, but Marta waves me off with a toss of her dark head.

"Oh, come on! It'll be fun playing detective." She looks at Don. "Can't the public ask them how they got their information?"

"Nope." His answer is cut and dried, and Marta almost droops in disappointment. "That's going to be part of the police report, and if it's not available because of an ongoing investigation, only journalists can request it. And that might not even work if they don't want to share at the moment," he says with a shrug.

The three of us sit in silence for a moment, each recalibrating our thoughts. Finally I stir and say, "Can't Chrissy ask? I mean, it's her house they came to. Shouldn't she at least be able to find out how they got her address?"

This is beginning to feel like a hamster wheel: around and around we go, the same questions appearing after each new revolution. We are back at question one. The only thing we've accomplished is to make coffee for a nosy journalist.

"Look, I've got a few contacts in the SLPD. Let me reach out and see what they have to say, okay?" Don takes the final sip of coffee, tilting his head back to get the last drop. "Man, we need this shit at the office. I could kill for a decent cup of coffee when I'm working."

"It's because you still use a communal pot," says Marta smugly, glancing over at our Keurig. "Get yourself a single server like I did. It's amazing what it can do."

Don snorts, standing up and carrying his empty mug over to the deep stainless steel sink. "Yeah, and as soon as my back's turned, some other reporter will confiscate it and claim it's his." He shakes his head in disgust. "I'll just keep stopping at Circle K every morning. At least their coffee's fresh."

He leaves with the promise to call as soon as he knows something. I'm skeptical. A newspaper writer probably wouldn't take time for a debriefing in the middle of the hunt. Marta, on the other hand, has more faith in the human animal than I do.

"Next time he drops by, we need to feed the man. He looks positively starved."

It's my turn to snort.

"He lives on cigarettes and coffee, love. Didn't you see him light it up as soon as he got back in that rattletrap of a van?"

I actually do his vehicle a disservice by calling it names. It's a classic, or soon will be, and he's obviously put some time and care into maintaining it. I remembered how my sister and I would play "slug bug," punching each other in the shoulder whenever we saw a Volkswagen Beetle. When we spotted a

Volkswagen van, though, we yelled "Twinkie!" and got to hit each other twice—and twice as hard. My mom hated it.

I tuck that memory away for later. I'll need to teach our child how to play. In the meantime, I need to focus on Marta. And murder. You know, just a typical day, dabbling in mayhem and hoping to make sense out of tragedy. That's beginning to feel like the modus operandi in our house.

With a fleeting thought for my sister, I follow my partner back inside, closing the door between us and the outside world.

Chapter Seven

The cacophony of barking and hissing is almost music to my ears. I'm back in the saddle, taking my turn at the monthly free veterinarian clinic Lou and I started a few years back. Our clients are mostly pets of the homeless population, although a few belong to families whose budget doesn't run to pet care.

I'm examining the ears of an indignant Siamese cat when I happen to glance up and spot the young man from the accident at the Vineyard. He is standing in line, cuddling a Yorkshire puppy in his arms, his eyes half closed as he nuzzles its soft fur. He's standing just behind a young girl and her mom, each of them holding a ferret. My heart picks up the pace a bit. I fully intend to use this opportunity to question him about Bev.

After diagnosing ear mites in the Siamese and giving the owner a handful of medicine samples, I send the ferrets over to my intern. The young man is standing right in front of me, his arms full of wriggling puppy. I listen as he explains the reason for coming here today, then I begin to examine the Yorkie.

"He's been like this since last week, and I'm starting to get worried. I mean, he always eats his food, so that's not the issue, but his stomach is always, I don't know, distended afterward." He's staring down anxiously at his pet, watching me as I gently prod the animal's sides and belly. I've already got an idea of the problem.

"Do you feed him anything other than dog food? Anything that might have a high fat content?" I gently pet the squirming puppy, watching him nip at his owner's fingers.

The young man blushes. "Well, I don't, but my friend might. She moved in a couple weeks ago, kind of a temporary thing. She likes to cook," he says with a sudden grin. "Even a full breakfast."

"Including things like bacon? Or maybe sausage?" I can picture the Yorkie, begging for bites.

He nods. "Yeah. And I think she's slipping him stuff when I'm not looking. I mean, who can resist? He's so cute, you know?"

"I'm pretty sure your dog's got a form of pancreatitis," I say as I hand him back to his owner. "It's not serious right now, but it could get that way if you're not careful. No more fat at all for this guy, okay? In fact, only feed him dog food formulated for his size. I don't care how cute he is." I reach out and ruffle the puppy's soft fur. "If you'll hang on a sec, I'll go back and get you a bag of the food I want you to use, okay?"

With a promise that he'll wait, I leave the examination area and head down the hallway to a small room near the back door. We keep clinic supplies here, along with free samples from companies that want us to promote their brands. I find the food I'm looking for and head back to where I left the young man and his Yorkie.

The two ferret owners are gone, and my intern is handling the last examination of the day. At first I can't see the Yorkie owner, then I spot him across the road, leaning against a older pickup. I can see the puppy peeking out of the driver's side window, licking at something on the outside of the truck.

He's going to have to watch this pup. I have a feeling it's an omnivorous animal that wouldn't turn down anything that vaguely resembles edible. I see many more instances of stomach issues in its future if he's not careful.

Crossing the road, I hold out the colorful bag of food. "Here you go. By the way, I didn't get your name. I'm Giselle Cutler."

"Rex," he says, turning around and placing the food in the open bed of the pickup. "I know who you are," he says almost casually. "My brother told me he talked to you at the restaurant."

Although I was going to bring up the fact that he already knew who I was before coming here today, it sets my nerves on edge. Still, I'm not going to ignore the opening.

"Yes," I agree. "Jinx, I think he said his name is."

Rex snorts. "Whatever. It's really Jeremy, but he thinks Jinx sounds better, that it fits him."

I laugh. "Well, I happen to agree. He certainly looks like a Jinx." I stop, considering a moment. "Maybe not a jinx, exactly, but…" I'm not making much sense, and I certainly don't want to offend his brother. Thankfully, Rex seems to be following my disjointed thoughts.

"He was definitely a jinx for poor Bev, I can tell you that much." He shakes his head. "Thank goodness she's all right."

"Ah. The woman who got injured in the parking lot." I hesitate, not wanting him to know just how linked to her I am. It's six degrees of separation minus four. "Is she a good friend?"

Rex's face lights up. The puppy yelps for attention, and he reaches in the window with one hand. "She's amazing, that's what. When I had my transplant thing, she stayed with me until I got back on my feet."

I'm missing a huge chunk of information here. I thought Jinx had said Rex had sold his bone marrow, not that he'd had a transplant.

"You're a transplant patient?"

"No, not a patient." The Yorkie is jumping up and down, trying to get his attention. Rex gives in and lifts him out, cradling him close to his chest. "I sold my bone marrow to this clinic, and Bev stayed over a few days until I felt better. It was a great way to make some cash, but it really takes it out of you for a while, you know?" He plants a kiss on top of the dog's head. "I gotta get going, Doc. Thanks for the food. And I'll tell Bev to stop giving him scraps."

"Wait," I say, putting out one hand to touch his arm. "Can I ask you how you know Bev?"

Rex looks at me for a moment as if considering his answer. "I ran into her at the dog park over on Fleming. She said she had a pet that died, and she liked to come and watch the dogs run around and stuff. We got to talking about Tramp here and got to be friends before you know it. It's a good thing, too, since she's the one who told me about the clinic."

Now his expression is curious, and I realize I can't go any farther with this conversation. Besides, I need to share this info with Marta and Chrissy, get their take on it. Bev Strait could simply be a Good Samaritan, wanting to help out a young man who is obviously struggling financially. My imagination, after all, sometimes takes on a life of its own.

"Well, I'm glad that you stopped by today. Tramp, did you say? That's a great name. Reminds me of that Disney film." I give Tramp's ears one more caress and step back from the truck as the motor fires up.

"Disney film?" Rex concentrates as he clips his seat belt into place. "I don't know about that. I just named him that because that's what we are. We're tramps." And with a throaty roar of the engine, he pulls away from the curb.

Marta is stretched out on the couch when I get home, her laptop balanced on her growing hump of stomach as she types rapidly. Without lifting her gaze from the screen, she says, "I picked up dinner from Bola Thai, love. Your food is in the microwave."

The strongly aromatic scent of spicy shrimp soup and the tang of red curry greets my senses, and my stomach growls an acknowledgment. When I am working, either at the office on a regular shift or with the free clinic, I tend to survive on coffee and more coffee. Trust Marta to have sustenance waiting for me.

"I was absolutely craving that soup earlier," she says as I come back into the living room, balancing my dinner and a can of sparkling water. "I figured we might as well have it for dinner." She looks up long enough to blow a kiss across the room before returning to her task.

So much for a loving partner who lives only for my comfort, I think with an inward smile. I start to say something sassy but then stop. Is this a harbinger of days to come? Will my needs become second place when the baby arrives? It's enough to dispel my hunger pangs. I take a half-hearted sip of the soup and let the spoon fall back into the bowl with an unnecessary clang.

"Is it too hot?" Marta sounds concerned, and she tries to sit up, leaning heavily on one elbow to help her maneuver. "I probably should have asked you first, Gij. Sorry."

"No, it's fine. The spoon just slipped." I grasp the offending utensil again and try for a contrite smile. "I didn't mean to interrupt whatever it is you're doing over there."

"Oh, that." Marta sets the laptop aside, waving it off with

one hand. "I was just trying to get the hang of that word search game everyone seems to be playing."

At least it's not more baby name searches. I'm okay with something easy to spell and pronounce, like Ann. Or Ava. My partner, though, tends to like names that have meanings. Like Abigail—"a joy to behold"—or Belinda, which means, so the website tells me, "very beautiful."

"So how'd you do?" I take a test sip of the soup and find it to be just right, very baby bearish. I'm Goldilocks, eating my way through a meal that most likely would have never appeared on the menu for the Bear family.

"I'm in seventh place," she says disgustedly. "You'd think I could beat an eighth grader at this, right?"

"You're playing against an eighth grader?" I scoop another mouthful of the broth and get a large piece of succulent shrimp. "How do you know?"

Marta shrugs. "I don't, I guess. Actually, it's probably one of those creepy men who still live in their parents' basement at forty."

I nod, a grimace on my face. "And collects action figures. You've got to be careful who you connect with online, love."

"I know, I know. And I tell my clients that all the time. Guess I need to listen to my own advice." She swings her legs over the side of the couch and sits up. "How was the clinic today?"

Instantly, an image of Rex and Tramp pops into my mind.

"You'll never guess who showed up," I say, standing up and heading to the kitchen.

"Santa Claus," she calls after me. "Or the Tooth Fairy."

"No, goofy." I walk back in to the living room and plop down on the end of the couch, curling up on my side in order to face her. "It was Rex."

"Rex? Rex who?"

"That waiter named Jinx, the one who dances all over the place? It's his brother. You know, the one who was with Bev Strait at the Vineyard." I don't add anything about the accident, but I can see Marta's mind going there. She frowns slightly as she puts the laptop on the floor and faces me.

"What are the odds?" She shakes her head, the frown still there.

"It's gotta be that universal thing again," I tease. But her attention is on something else. "What, love?"

"It's just too weird, Gij. How is it all these people we seem to run across are already connected? Chrissy, Bev, Jinx, and now Rex." She ticks the names off on her fingers, drawing her eyebrows together. "I can't even see a common denominator here."

"Bone marrow. No, hang on," I say as she begins to protest. "Didn't Jinx say his brother sold his for profit? And didn't Chrissy say she had a transplant when she was a kid?"

"That might just be coincidence, Gij. It's not unique to have a transplant anymore."

"But it is when we come across four people in as many days, all of whom seem to be attached not just to transplants but specifically to bone marrow. Now, that's plain ol' weird, however you look at it."

"How does Bev fit into all of this?" Marta's expression is skeptical, a role I usually play.

"That's even stranger. Rex told me he met her at the dog park, they got to talking, and she ended up asking him if he'd like to make some easy money."

Marta rolls her eyes. "Let me guess. She told him where he could go to sell his bone marrow. Gij, do you know just how idiotic that sounds? Bev is one of the most straitlaced people I know. There's no way she'd encourage someone to do anything like that."

"Is it illegal to sell your bone marrow?" I'm interested now, and I jerk my chin at the laptop. "Look it up, okay? I'm curious."

After just a few minutes, we discover that as of January 2014, a federal court allowed the sale of bone marrow in nine states, including California. And it's a lucrative, if highly governed, industry.

"You can get that much? Good grief," Marta says, running both hands through her dark hair. "We're in the wrong business, Gij."

I slump back on the couch, trying to reconcile the idea that Bev might be involved in something semi-shady. A gray market. "Do you think there might be, I don't know, moral issues with Bev? I mean, she's a state employee, right? Doesn't that fall along the lines of moral turpitude or something?"

"I don't know." Marta's voice is troubled, her gaze on her hands. "Isn't that a topic for Chrissy? She's the boss, after all."

I shrug. "Probably. Speaking of Chrissy, I wonder if Don's found out anything about that body."

Marta smacks her forehead with the palm of one hand. "Oh, I'm such an idiot! I completely forgot to tell you." She gets off the couch and heads to the small table in the entryway, coming back with something in her hand. "He came by earlier and dropped this off for you." She smiles as she hands me a long, white envelope. "Sorry, love. Blame it on the preggo brain."

Without comment, which seems to be the safest move, I slip the tip of one finger under the loose end of the envelope's gummed flap. I manage to get the contents out with only the slightest of paper cuts, sticking the offended digit in my mouth as I flatten the sheet of paper out and begin to read.

When I am finished, the cut and Marta's forgetfulness

are ancient history. Don Butler has certainly lived up to his reputation with this little gem. I silently pass the letter to Marta.

"How in the world did he find that out?"

Marta's mouth is hanging open in a most unlovely fashion, but I know my own is a mirror image. Don's research has uncovered something that could lead to an international crisis. It would definitely be catastrophic for Bev Strait if this got into the wrong hands.

"It's what investigative reporters do, love. They investigate stuff. They find out things some people don't want uncovered." I shake my head, looking back down at the letter. "Something like this would be a bombshell. I'm pretty sure it's frowned upon to sell organs to other countries."

"I can't believe Bev would be involved in something like that, Gij. I just can't." Marta's dark eyes are troubled, and she puts one hand on her belly, unconsciously hugging it in a protective gesture. I don't blame her. This is a world I'm not crazy about myself. It gives the entire situation an R-rated movie flavor, black market, murder, and all. I want to raise my child in a G-rated world, thank you very much.

"Keep in mind he says he's still checking out a few more leads." I wave the letter and let it fall onto my lap. "And he's got a meeting with a contact in the medical field tonight. Hopefully, we'll have more information after that."

Marta leans back against the rolled arm of the couch, eyes closed and hands clasped behind her head. She has dark bruising under each eye, telling me she's still not resting as much as she should.

"Tell you what, babe, let's get you under the covers and have an early evening. We can read or do whatever your little heart desires. How's that sound?"

She smiles, eyes still shut.

"I'll take that as a yes." I stand up, careful to put the letter back in the envelope. If this becomes a legal issue, I want proof I am on the honorable side of things. "Want a lift?"

This time her eyes fly open, already in the middle of a roll. Clearly my suggestion isn't welcome. I give her a sassy grin and head for the stairs.

CHAPTER EIGHT

Monday morning arrives too soon. Marta gets ready for work without any adverse reaction, but I'm dragging my feet as I head down the stairs into the kitchen. I blindly jab at the Keurig and place an earthenware mug under the spout. Hopefully, a shot of caffeine will help my "get up and go" get up and get out of here.

"Will you button this for me?"

I turn, steaming mug in hand, and see Marta in what can only be described as maternity clothes. She's wearing a loose blouse that hangs over a pair of cropped pants, both in a vibrant shade of lemon yellow. She looks absolutely lovely. Head turning, heart stopping.

"Nice rags," I say, striving for casual as my heart threatens to fly from my chest, an addlepated bird in spring. I love this woman so much, and watching her gradually morph into an unmistakably pregnant woman is breathtaking. "Turn around."

I can't help it. I drop a kiss on the side of her neck.

"Don't start something you can't finish," she says teasingly, looking over her shoulder with twinkling eyes. "Besides, I want to be a little early this morning, especially since it seems all hell's broken out since I've been gone."

"Isn't that the truth?" I give her back a final pat and turn back to the coffee maker. "Want a green tea to go?"

The house is almost too quiet after she leaves, promising to get something to eat on her way into the office. I sit at the kitchen table with another cup of coffee at my elbow and a plate of toast in front of me. I've recently discovered the phenomenon that is avocado toast, and I've spread a generous amount of spicy guacamole on each slice of bread. Marta laughs at me when I do this, joking that I'm not a purist when it comes to food. I don't care. Guacamole can jazz up anything, including breakfast, and since it's made of avocado, I figure it's kosher.

I've just finished rinsing my plate and mug when my cell phone begins its journey across the table, vibrating as I get an incoming call. I almost dive for it, afraid it's Marta and something's wrong.

"Giselle Cutler," I say into the mouthpiece, trying to control my breathing so I don't sound out of breath or out of shape.

"It's Don." I can hear something rustling on his end of the line. "Got a minute or three?"

"Sure." I sink down into a chair and try to rein in my rapid heartbeat. "What's up?"

"Well, it'll make more sense if we do this face-to-face," he says. "Want to meet somewhere?"

"Sure." I think quickly, trying to decide on a place that will be close to the clinic. I don't want to be late, either. "How about San Leandro Café? In fifteen?"

"Sounds good." With a click, he's gone.

The San Leandro Café is part of a burgeoning mom-and-pop scene in our town, owned and manned by a local extended family. I'm a huge fan of their biscuits and gravy platter—the greasier the better, in my opinion—while Marta leans toward the vegetarian omelet, complete with a side of fruit and melba toast. And I enjoy supporting a locally owned business. I remind myself about this, even though I've already eaten breakfast. I can't let the local economy down, can I? By the time Don has joined me, I'm already nursing a mug of coffee and waiting on my virtuous half order of biscuits and gravy.

"Morning." Don Butler settles into the booth across from me as the vinyl cushion gives out a rude welcome. I choose to ignore it, although I catch a muted giggle from the two children sitting nearby with their dour-faced parents. Nothing like fart noises to entertain the younger crowd.

"Good morning." I nod at the legal notepad in his hand, a blue pen jammed into the spiral at the top. "What've you got for me?"

"Well, I got more information last night. My contact," he says as he begins to flip through the pages, "tells me she knows the details behind an organ-selling scheme. One that's bigger than the local scene, she says."

I smile up at the waitress when she delivers my second breakfast. "Don, do you want anything? Coffee?"

He shakes his head. "I'm good. Just water, please."

I almost feel guilty when I take the first bite of sausage-laden gravy and fluffy biscuit. Almost.

"Is there anything that links Marta's boss with the, you know, the medical situation?" I'm hesitant to use names and find myself speaking in semi-code. I know I sound idiotic, and I flush. Don grins across at me, obviously finding my attempt at subterfuge amusing.

"Are you asking if Chrissy Burton's a part of the organ transplant community, besides being a bone marrow recipient?" He shrugs and takes a sip of water. "What I do know is Beverly Strait gets a finder's fee for each person she sends to the donor's clinic."

I chew and swallow, giving myself time to process this information. This is beginning to sound bigger than anything I want to become involved with.

"A finder's fee. That's interesting." I don't know what else to say. "Do we know how she got involved in this?"

Don nods, flipping back a few pages in his notebook. "According to my source, she was a volunteer at the hospital that does the transplants. I'm not sure who got her tangled up in recruiting donors, but it's gotta be someone there."

"You mean someone at the hospital asked Bev to enlist people to sell their bone marrow?" I give an involuntary shudder. "That's creepy."

"Right?" Don's smile is sharklike, wide and toothy. "Almost smacks of Hollywood."

Visions of zombies and body parts flit into my mind, and I swallow a bite of sausage with difficulty. I'm definitely not a gory movie person, despite the surgeries I've performed at the clinic. That's the real world. Selling one's organs definitely feels like a horror flick.

"Are we talking just bone marrow or something else?" I can feel my shoulders slowly rising toward my ears, tension working its way across my back. I force myself to relax. It can't be that bad.

Another shrug. "From what I understand, it's bone marrow and anything else you can part with, like kidneys. Even lobes from livers and lungs."

"That's hard to believe." I protest. "This is the Bay Area, not some third world country."

"All the more reason to trot out the capitalistic experience." Don's eyebrows, dark in comparison to his sparse hair, are drawn together. "Any ol' way to make a buck or three."

We sit in silence for a few minutes, each of us focused on our own thoughts.

"So, is there anything that can help identify the woman in the bay?" I ask the question even before I really think the words. And I'm not sure why my mind has gone in this direction.

"Are you talking an organ connection? Or information?"

It's my turn to shrug. "No clue. Sorry, that just popped into my head."

"Interestingly enough, yes." He closes the notebook and flips it back and forth between nicotine-stained fingers. "She actually had a transplant recipient's card on her, which is how they came to ID her as your gal's boss."

"You're joking." This is becoming more and more convoluted, a bad script full of any and all clichés. "How in the world..." I let my words hang in the air between us as the waitress swings by and slaps the bill down.

"No hurry, hon. I can be your cashier or you can take it up to the front."

"Thanks," I say with a smile. "I'll take it up."

With a swish of her polyester uniform and a smile, she's off to dispense coffee and sunshine and bills to other customers.

"As you were saying?" Don nods, watching me over the rim of the glass as he takes another drink of water.

"I was just trying to figure out how someone could have gotten Chrissy's card. I mean, isn't that something she'd be carrying with her for life?"

"You would think. Of course, I've got a theory."

"And?"

"Well, let's suppose that the dead woman was connected somehow to this Bev Strait." I begin to protest the absurdity of the idea, but he holds up his hands. "No, hear me out, Dr. Cutler. We now know Bev was a volunteer at the hospital. And we also know her boss is a transplant recipient. And adopted.

Let's just imagine other siblings out there have the same medical issues and need a transplant as well." He pauses, and I give him an impatient nod, waiting to hear the rest.

"So, let's pretend Bev happened to come across this woman at the hospital, made a connection, and somehow got hold of her boss's card with the intention of making a comparison. The woman takes the card, sees the possibility of finding a long-lost sister, and voilà, we have the perfect setup for murder. Or depression. She could've jumped in herself after being rejected. It's a well-known fact some adopted adults don't take kindly to being discovered."

I can't help laughing.

"So, now you're suggesting Chrissy Burton is a killer. And she killed her sister because she didn't want a relationship." I shake my head, ignoring the curious glances from those seated nearby. "Marta's a great judge of character, and there's no way she'd work for someone like that."

Don gives a half shrug. "As I said, it's just a theory."

I cross my arms on the table and lean forward, lowering my voice. "Well, let's set her up, see what she has to say about this idea of yours."

"Exactly what I was going to suggest." Now his face is a mass of lines as he smiles widely at me. "You up for a little acting?"

"If it helps to settle things down at my partner's workplace. The last thing she needs right now is to be dealing with drama." I reach for the bill and wave it at Don like a matador's cape. "And just to show how glad you are to have me on board, you can get this."

His snort would make any bull jealous.

❖

The clinic keeps me and Lou busy, a virtual parade of pets moving through the reception area and back to the various examination rooms. Before the morning is half over, I've diagnosed pregnancy in a Great Dane, hip dysplasia in an older dachshund, symptoms of diabetes in a Persian cat, and fleas in a ferret. I write scripts for prenatal vitamins and a back leg sling to relieve the hip issues, order glucose tests, and recommend a bath using flea soap. When I take a moment to update my files during a short lull in the action, I notice my cell phone's screen is flashing silently at me. I've got several text messages waiting to be read, one from a number I don't recognize.

Just wanted to let you know I ate this morning. A breakfast burrito, no less, and it stayed down. XOXO. Marta's text makes me smile, and I rapidly text back a reply.

Sounds good, luv. Busy here but should be home by 5. XO times infinity.

My nephew Leif has sent me a meme depicting the latest political commentary. I send him an emoticon with its tongue hanging out and eyes crossed. Politics can take a flying leap as far as I'm concerned.

I open the text from the unknown number. I stare at the screen, reading and rereading the short message. Only four words in length, but the words carry a weighty message: *Stay away from Bev.*

"Dr. Cutler, there's a canine vaccination waiting for you in three." I look up from my phone and see the new receptionist standing there, concern on her face. "Is everything all right? I mean, is your partner okay?" Lou hired her in my absence last fall, and I still haven't learned her name. I try to read her name badge without that obvious squint thing I find myself doing more and more often, but no go.

"She's fine, thanks." I give myself a mental shake, forcing

my attention back to the here and now. "Can you ask Dr. Grafton to take it? I need to make a phone call."

Without waiting for an answer, I head for the small office Lou and I share. It's just big enough for two desks placed face-to-face, each with a filing cabinet behind it and one shared bookshelf. Closing the door, I sink into the ergonomic chair Marta gave me for my birthday, a bumpy-looking contrivance surprisingly comfortable to use. Calling up my contacts list, I hit the icon beside Don Butler's name, drumming my fingers impatiently on the desktop as I wait for him to answer.

When I get his voice mail, I'm tempted to hang up rather than listening to his self-serving message. I wait, though, holding the phone away from my ear until I hear the high-pitched beep.

"Don, this is Giselle Cutler. Call me as soon as you get this message." I hesitate and add a gruff thanks before disconnecting.

I toss the cell phone down and clasp my hands behind my head, my gaze on the ceiling. Who knew we talked about Bev and her part in this fiasco? Closing my eyes, I ran through the past two days, trying to think.

There was Chrissy Burton, of course, but it doesn't make sense for her to warn me away, not when she asked for help. Jinx is a maybe, as he might have mentioned to his brother something about our conversation concerning his bone marrow "donation." Rex, of course, is a possibility. I asked enough questions to make him suspicious, including something about Bev.

And then there was Bev herself. She had three different contacts who could each tell her about my concern with her part in the organ transplant community. Any one of these four could find out my cell number, especially since it's listed as an emergency number for after hours. Marta has mentioned this before, citing exactly a scenario such as this one.

"You don't need to post your personal contact info, Gij. Just get an answering service. Or set the clinic's number to ring to you when the clinic's closed."

I'm beginning to see the sense in that suggestion, something that's never been an issue before this.

I'm scrolling through Google, trying to ascertain just how much a reliable answering service will cost when my cell phone begins to sing, Queen's "Bohemian Rhapsody" announcing an incoming call.

"Giselle Cutler," I say, and I'm relieved to hear Don's voice on the other end.

"You sounded stressed on your voice mail." I can hear others talking in the background, the sounds of a busy newsroom intruding on our conversation. "Hang on a sec. I need to get somewhere a bit less chaotic."

I can hear movement, then the sound of a door opening and closing, effectively shutting out the circus outside.

"There, that's better." A chair creaks as Don sits down, followed by a thump I can only imagine are his feet landing on top of a desk. "You'd think there were a hundred people out there, not just ten. Now, what's up?"

I tell him about the text message. Has he received one as well?

"Not that I'm aware of," he says, "but I get all kinds of crank messages."

"I don't think this one is a crank, Don. It's too close to our conversation this morning." I swing my chair around and face the window, staring out at the small courtyard just behind the clinic. "Either someone overheard us and wants to play games, or someone followed us there."

"Or someone's taking a stab in the dark, trying to rattle your cage."

I let that idea hang there for a minute, running through the Rolodex in my mind. Who do I know that would do something like that?

"I don't know," I finally say. "It feels too close to the issue, not like someone's idea of a joke." I watch one of the clinic's assistants, a shaggy-haired college student who has stepped outside for a quick smoke break, arms crossed over his body in an attempt to stay warm. "Personally, I'm leaning toward the scenario that someone out there doesn't want us to get any closer to the whole organ donor thing."

"And I'm inclined to think that as well." His voice is sober, underpinned with concern rather than the eagerness I would have expected. "In fact, I'm thinking we need to give what we have to the police and wash our hands of the whole thing."

A brief memory of Chrissy Burton's tearstained face flashed across my mind. I promised I'd help her get to the bottom of things. Backing out now would make me feel guilty. On the other hand, I might live a bit longer.

Before I have a chance to voice these thoughts, the door to my office opens, and the receptionist peers into the room. This time I get a better look at her badge. Maxine, I think it says.

"Dr. Cutler," she says, concern on her face, "we've got a situation out here. Someone named Jinx is refusing to leave until he sees you."

Fabulous. The clinic is becoming a meet and greet. First, Rex and now Jinx. If Bev and Chrissy show up, we'll have a complete set.

"Can you send him back here? I'm still in the middle of something." I point to my cell phone, conscious Don can hear what is being said.

She nods, a bemused look. She's too polite to ask, although I can imagine the conversation among my employees. Thank goodness for Lou. She'll put a screeching halt to anything with even a whiff of gossip.

"It looks like I've got a visitor, Don. Do you want to continue this later or hang on until I see what it's all about?"

"I can hang," he says. "I've got some emails I need to check anyway."

I can hear rapid footsteps just outside my door again, and I turn around in time to see Jinx slip around the door, his expression troubled. I don't need to be psychic to know this won't be a friendly visit. Something else has happened, and it's not good.

"Have a seat," I say, waving at Lou's empty chair across from me. "Can I get you anything? A water?"

He shakes his head silently, and it occurs to me he simply walked in, all signs of his signature twirling gone. I hesitate a moment, an idea forming.

"Jinx, would it be all right with you if I put a friend of mine on speakerphone? I have a feeling he'll want to hear this as well."

Jinx shrugs, still silent.

"Okay, here we go." I push the icon for speaker and lay the phone on my desk. "Don, I've got Jinx here. He's Rex's brother, the one I was telling you about. Jinx, this is Don Butler." I purposely leave out Don's title, aware it might shut Jinx down even more.

"Hey, Jinx. Dr. Cutler tells me you know about the bone marrow donations, right?"

Across from me, Jinx makes a derisive sound. "Donate, my shiny hiney!"

I hear Don convert a laugh into a cough at Jinx's words, and I have to look down to hide a smile.

"My brother wouldn't give water to a thirsty saint. It's all about the money with him."

"Is that what you're here to talk about?" Don has taken over the conversation, and I lean back in my chair, content to be an observer for the moment. He is a seasoned investigator, after all, and something like this is right up his alley.

"Sort of." Jinx shifts in the chair, glancing up from the phone to me. "I wanted to tell the doc about something I overheard last night. It's been bugging me, and I just need to get it off my chest."

"Which was?" I say, steepling my fingers under my chin.

Jinx pauses, either trying to choose his words or debating how much to say. I try not to be annoyed, but I'm suddenly anxious to get as much information as possible. I want an end to this entire debacle. I want to be able to concentrate on my life without the specter of murder hanging over my head.

"Okay, so, you know how Rex did the whole bone marrow thing, and that woman Bev stayed with him," Jinx says to me. "Well, it seems Miss Nosy has decided to move in permanently with him. She's practically taking over his life!" He sounds indignant now, and it's hard for me to feel bad for him. If he's interrupted my day to tattle on his brother's private life, I'll be very irritated.

"And why do you think this is important?" Don breaks in, his tone brusque.

"Because she's the one in charge of the whole gimme-your-organs thing. And I don't want my brother involved with someone so *ghoulish*." Jinx sounds truly upset, his voice rising as he speaks. I stand up and push the door closed. I don't need the rest of the office hearing this conversation.

"How is she in charge?" I lean forward, careful to lower my voice. Hopefully, Jinx will mirror my tone and calm down.

He swipes at his eyes with the back of one hand.

"Well, she keeps a laptop and printer at his place, and Rex told me she uses them to schedule appointments for 'prospective clients.'" Jinx quirks his fingers in air quotes, disgust in his movements. "Like she's a big-shot business gal or something. I personally think it's gross, selling body parts. I mean, shouldn't everyone have to wait in line?"

Don and I both start to speak at the same time.

"Go ahead, Don," I say, pushing a small pack of tissues across to Jinx. He's clearly very upset, close to tears again.

"Let me just get this clear, Jinx. You say Bev is running an organ donation business from Rex's house, and she's selling these donations to people in need of transplants."

"He doesn't have a house, just a tiny apartment," says Jinx. "And yeah, that's exactly what's she's doing."

"Uh, isn't that just slightly illegal?" I ask into the silence following Jinx's statement.

"I'm looking that up as we speak," says Don, and I can hear the sound of rapid clicking from his end of the line. Jinx and I wait in silence until Don gives a muted grunt. "Okay, it says here, and I quote, 'Only one country allows an open market of buying organs from living donors. Iran, however, does limit these purchases to its own citizens in an effort to control the market.'"

"You're kidding." I'm stumped, to be honest. I'm amazed anyone allows this type of trade, much less one of the stricter religious countries in the entire world. "So, I take it that it's a big no-no here in the good ol' U S of A?"

"You would be correct." I hear Don shuffling paper in the background, and I can imagine he's writing in his notebook. "Look, Jinx. Is there a good time for us to meet up?"

Jinx's eyes widen slightly, and he stares at me as if I'm the one to give him permission. I nod and smile encouragingly at him.

"He's a nice guy," I say to Jinx. "Doesn't bite, likes coffee, and will pay for any information you give him. Isn't that right, Don?"

Don snorts. "Oh, sure. I'll at least buy the coffee. So, whaddya say? Are you available this evening? Or would tomorrow morning be better?"

I'll say one thing for Don Butler. When he gets the bit between his teeth, he's full steam ahead.

"Um, tonight? I have to work in the morning."

"Sounds good. Where would you like to meet? It's your call."

"How about the Turf Club?" Jinx grins suddenly, a sassy expression on his face. "It's not far from here, just down in Hayward."

"I know where it is, thanks." Don's tone is dry, causing me and Jinx to laugh. "Say about eight?"

"I'll be the one in sequins." Jinx's voice is thick with laughter. I can imagine the expression on Don's face, and I smile.

Don disconnects the call and Jinx stands up, holding out one hand to me. "Thanks, Doc, for seeing me. I appreciate it."

I hug him instead, and I can feel just how thin he is. He reminds me of Marta, both of them delicate under my hands, their bones avian and hollow.

"No problem." I pull back from him and smile. "Did you have to pick the campest gay bar?"

"Why, yes indeedy." Jinx flutters his lashes at me, hands resting on his slim hips. "A boy's gotta get his fun somewhere, right?"

I shake my head as I retrieve my phone and replace it in my lab coat pocket.

"Just be nice. And don't scare him."

"Moi? Surely you jest." He winks at me, his emotional

equilibrium apparently restored. I give an exaggerated sigh and motion him out of the office ahead of me. I have a feeling Don is in for a wild ride tonight, courtesy of Jinx.

The rest of the day flies by, and I'm almost surprised when five o'clock hits. I'm tired, though, and I'm looking forward to a relaxing evening with Marta. I haven't heard from her at all, which is a bit unexpected, but I'm sure her day has been chaotic at best.

Leaving instructions for the office staff to forward the calls to my cell phone, my stopgap plan until I get a messaging service, I head out to the parking lot. The evening breezes have sprung up, and the pungent scent of eucalyptus is in the air. My office is surrounded by a stand of these stately trees, their branches providing a home to what seems like a million cawing birds.

Tonight, though, they are silent, almost eerily so. The edges of fog beginning to roll in behind the light winds give a slightly macabre cast to the dying light, and I shiver as I click the fob to unlock the CRV.

Of course, I could have simply put my hand in through the broken window.

CHAPTER NINE

The officer who arrives to take the report is kind, making sure I've called my insurance already and I know when the official report will be available.

"This is a fairly quiet area, to be honest," he says as he caps his pen and replaces it in his breast pocket. "I'm kinda surprised you didn't hear your alarm go off when the glass broke."

I can feel my face flush, and I'm glad it's getting dark outside.

"It's been on the blink lately, going off at random times for no reason, so I guess I disconnected it." I give a shrug, trying to play it off. Truthfully, I'm afraid my insurance company isn't going to be quite as understanding when I have to admit this.

"Well, that might cause a little bit of snag, but you need a window." He holds out his hand and shakes mine firmly. "Try to have a better evening, Doc."

I certainly plan on it.

The drive home is chilly, damp tendrils of the bay fog reaching into the Honda. I can already hear Marta, although I might need to remind her I unhooked the damn thing for her sake. Every time she finally fell asleep, the alarm would begin its incessant blaring. If I can get her talking about her day, I might be able to conveniently forget to tell her until later. Like next year.

In the meantime, I'm debating whether this was a random stroke of bad luck or something more sinister. Perhaps it's a warning, a cautionary message telling me I need to back away from investigating any more. Or maybe it's just my turn to be the victim of a crime. This is the Bay Area, after all. Anything can happen here and most usually does.

My house is lit up like a Christmas tree when I pull up to the curb. Marta has a habit of turning on every light as she passes through each room. I usually come behind her and turn them off again. We are the yin and yang of conservation, balancing out what could be a very large electric bill each month.

Marta's car is typically parked in the detached garage with me behind it in the driveway, but I'm going to need to park inside until I get the window fixed. Which means I'll have to tell her about the whole ugly incident much sooner than I'd prefer.

I decide not to say a single word about the lights.

I can hear sounds from the kitchen as I shut the front door behind me. The tantalizing aroma of garlic greets me, and I can't help smiling. Marta is cooking again. Thank goodness, since my limited store of culinary skills was used up long ago.

"Hey, there," she says from the stovetop, turning around and giving me a smile. "Hope you're hungry. I've got manicotti with ricotta in the oven and a ton of garlic-infused veggies almost ready."

I walk up and slip my arms around her waist, or where her waist used to be. It's grown right along with her belly, and I'm amazed to notice how much it's expanded in such a short time.

Mr. Flores's unwelcome prediction floats into my mind, and I kick it out just as fast. I am not going there.

"If you're cooking it, I'll eat it." I drop a kiss on her shoulder and step back, leaning against the counter as I watch her expertly stirring the vegetables simmering in a large skillet. "So, tell me about your day. Was Chrissy there?"

Marta taps the spoon on the side of the skillet and lays it on a tile trivet. "Yes, much to my surprise. I honestly thought she'd be out trying to figure out how she was mistaken for that dead woman."

"Ah. That." I give her a sheepish smile. "I might have some idea of how that happened. Remember Jinx?"

"Yes. And he's involved in this great revelation how?"

"Can you sit down for a minute or so?" I motion to the kitchen table. "I've got quite a bit to tell you."

"Sure," she says, turning down the gas flame under the vegetables. "Start talking." She playfully shakes a finger at me. "And leave nothing out."

Great.

"Jinx stopped by this morning and had quite a few interesting things to say." I repeat the conversation as close to verbatim as I can, ending with the "date" he and Don have this evening.

"I have a feeling ol' Don is going to get an eyeful," I say with a shake of my head.

"No kidding. From what I recall, Jinx is quite the drama queen." She begins to rise but I put out a hand to stop her. I might as well get it over.

"But wait, there's more." I use my best imitation of a TV salesman and coax a smile out of her. It's a wary smile, though. Marta knows me too well. "I'll need to park in the garage just for tonight, at least until I get a window replaced."

"What happened, Gij? Are you okay?" She looks me over with anxious eyes, making sure I've not been cut by breaking glass.

"I'm fine. And I already made the police report and called the insurance. It was broken while I was in the clinic." I mentally cross my fingers she won't think to mention the obvious.

"Why didn't the alarm go off?"

She wouldn't be Marta if she didn't ask. I sigh, trying for a remorseful expression.

"You might not remember this, but I kinda disconnected it a few weeks back. It was going off for no reason, and I was afraid it would disrupt your sleep." There. Hangdog eyes, contrite tone. That should get her.

"You 'kinda' disconnected it?" Her air quotes let me know just how irked she is. "Gij, that's the most ignorant thing I've heard you say in a long time."

"Well, I guess I could've let it keep blaring." My hackles are up, and I'm beginning to feel just a tad self-righteous. I did it for her, willing to risk the possibility of something like this happening.

All right, maybe that last point is a bit over the top. I should have remembered to hook the thing back up. I'm not about to admit it, though. Instead, I watch as she gets up from the table and all but stomps over to the stove. If I don't take a helping of humble pie along with the manicotti, I could be in for one long night.

"Marta," I begin hesitantly, knowing how bitter the next words will taste, "will it help if I say that you're right and I'm wrong?" She looks at me, and I see the glare has been dimmed to almost normal. "Sorry I upset you. Really."

She gives me a one-fingered response along with a smile.

Later, after I've moved my car into the garage and parked

Marta's in the driveway, careful to set the alarm, we cuddle on the couch like two kids on a date. I've slipped one of our favorite movies into the DVD player and made a batch of popcorn, not quite walking on eggshells but close enough to be extra solicitous. Marta eats it up, both the popcorn and the attention. I let her, glad to be out of the proverbial doghouse. This sofa can be uncomfortable for someone as tall as I am.

When I arrive the next morning, the clinic is literally teeming with life. Someone has abandoned a very pregnant cat on the doorstep, and she's given birth in the lobby. Lou has arrived before me as usual, and she's kneeling besides the box someone commandeered for the mewling family.

"Well, looked what the cat dragged in," she says, nodding at the box. "Got a few minutes for a mommy checkup?"

"Sure, no prob." I take a peek over Lou's shoulder. At least eight tiny bodies crowd together, the small blind faces rooting against their mom's side. I can't even imagine trying to parent more than one child at a time. I could never be a cat. "Let me get set up for the day, and I'll get right on it."

By nine, I've examined the mother and the babies, seven females and one lone male in the bunch. Judging by their markings, daddy must have been Siamese. They'll be beautiful animals.

"Lou, I've got an idea." I walk into our shared office, wiping my newly washed hands on a wad of paper towels. "How about we put them in the reception area and see if we can get folks interested in adopting?"

"Sounds good to me." Lou looks up from her iPad, dual lines of worry between her eyebrows. "Giselle, what do you know about someone named Rex?"

The name takes me by surprise.

"Let's see. Yorkie pup by the name of Tramp, likes to eat lots of fatty food, prone to pancreatitis. The dog, not the man."

I edge closer to her desk, peering down at the screen in front of her. "Why?"

"I was checking messages from last evening, and we had a disturbing voice mail from someone by that name." Lou prefers a written transcript of any messages left for the clinic, hence the iPad. She looks at me, her gray eyes steady. "He asked for you."

"Oh, that." I give a short laugh meant to sound casual, but it comes out strangled. "I gave him some dog food when he came by the free clinic this weekend. What's he doing, asking for more already?"

She shakes her head, a half smile on her lips. "Actually, he said he had something for you. As in who broke your car window. Any idea what he might be talking about?"

"Unfortunately, yes." I shove both hands into the pockets of my lab coat. "When I left last night, the driver's side front window of the CRV was smashed in." I shrug. "Hey, we're just lucky it hasn't happened more often." Nodding toward her iPad, I ask, "So who does he say did it?"

"He didn't say. He wants you to contact him when you have a minute."

"Ha. He'll have to get in line. I need to get a mobile glass replacement here first, plus Marta wants me to double-check her ultrasound appointment." I grin, heading for the door. "And this place isn't going to run itself, chica. Let's get out there and be superheroes."

"I hear ya." Lou pushes the chair back with her substantial legs, slipping the iPad into a side drawer. "I'll take even rooms and you can have odds. Kinda like you."

"Oh, ha and double ha." Still, I'm smiling as I head down the hallway toward room one where a pregnant guinea pig and her nervous owner are waiting to hear if the babies are all right. Hopefully, I'll have some time around midmorning to make those phone calls. I put Rex and his message to the back of my mind and greet the first client of the day.

It's nearly noon by the time Lou and I have seen all of our patients. Even now, after several successful years, it still amazes me enough concerned pet owners have the wherewithal to bring their precious fur children to a see a vet. In this economy, when luxuries go by the wayside for most folks, our clinic is still thriving.

The window has been replaced. I decide to take a break outside, maybe snap a picture to send to Marta. I still need to contact the ultrasound folks and call Rex. We keep a set of lounger chairs on the back patio of the clinic, and I sit down gratefully, aware my capacity for standing long hours isn't what it used to be. How Lou does it, particularly with her girth, is a mystery.

As I finish the phone call for the ultrasound appointment, I hear footsteps in the narrow alley that runs behind the clinic. It's not an especially salubrious place to take a walk, and no one should be back there anyhow. I hesitate, wondering if I should dash back inside or wait to see who it is.

Curiosity wins out over common sense. Curiosity also killed the cat. I should have gone inside.

When the first shot ricochets off the clinic's wall, I am frozen in place. When the second buries itself in the ground just front of me, I am up and running, a frightened deer leaping for cover. Slamming in through the back door, I dive for cover into my office and straight into Lou's arms.

"Giselle! Are you all right?" Her moon face is creased in concern, eyes wide. "Someone's already called the cops."

"Someone just shot at me." My voice is shaking and so are my legs.

"Are you certain? This is the Bay Area, after all." She gives me a wry smile and a pat on my arm. "Unless there's a hit out on you, I'd guess it was random."

I know she's trying to calm me, to steer my emotions away from the edge. Still, I can feel angry tears in my eyes, and I want to punch something. First the window and now this.

"It didn't feel random." I swipe at my eyes with the back of one hand. "In fact, it felt pretty damn personal. Whoever it was hit the wall just behind me and the ground in front of me. That doesn't feel random, Lou."

She looks at me for a moment, her bottom lip caught between her teeth. This is the signal she's mulling over something important.

"Okay, let's say it was purposeful. Who would want to shoot at you?"

Before I have time to respond, the receptionist comes hurrying down the hallway.

"The cops are here. Want them to come back to the office?" Her face is paler than usual, contrasting the dark bangs on her forehead with her complexion. I might have been the one targeted, but everyone in the clinic is affected. And I can finally read her name badge. It's Maxi. Not Maxine.

"That's a good idea," I say, trying to conjure up a smile. "And if we don't have any more appointments, maybe we should close down for the day. Lou?" I turn to her for confirmation and she nods.

"I'll get right on it." Maxi looks slightly relieved. I'm sure she just wants to get out of here and get home. I know I do.

The two officers who arrive to take our report look vaguely familiar. I might have seen them around town, since San Leandro is not a very large place.

"So, we meet again." One of the officers, the first one down the hall, gives me a smile and then the penny drops.

These officers responded at the Vineyard when Bev Strait was injured.

"I promise you, I'm not always involved in stuff like this," I say as we shake hands. "Thanks for getting here so quickly. Would you like to come into the office?" I gesture to the open door behind me. "I can bring in a couple more chairs."

"No, that's okay," the first officer says. "This won't take too long." He turns to Lou. "Were you out there when the shots were fired?"

She shakes her head. "No, I was in here, going over some paperwork while I ate my lunch." She motions to me with her chin. "Dr. Cutler was the only one out there."

They pose a few more questions and send her out to sit with those in the front office. I take my seat and point to Lou's chair across the room.

"If one of you wants to sit there, I'm sure Dr. Grafton won't mind."

They both shake their heads, and the one whose badge says "S. King" points to his dark uniform pants.

"No offense, but it takes forever to get animal hair off these things." His smile is wide, easy. I can see the edge of an old flip phone peering from the front pocket of his shirt, a testimony to either frugality or low pay. I have a feeling I know which it is. Those willing to put their lives on the line for the rest of us are notoriously underpaid and overworked.

We go over the facts, the footsteps, the shots. I tell them about the broken car window and the message from Rex, and they exchange a glance.

"It's a long story, Officers. The weird part is that it's sort of related to that incident at the restaurant, the woman who was injured in the parking lot."

"Well, that's what we're here for, to find out what's going on, Doctor." Officer King looks at his partner, nods to the doorway. "Do you want to go outside and check out the wall and the ground? I'll get her statement and then join you."

"It might take a while," I say, trying to sound jovial. "It's been a little crazy lately."

"I've heard crazy before, trust me." He takes a small recorder out of his back pocket, putting it on the desk in front of me. "I'm going to record this just because it's easier, okay?"

I nod and take in a deep breath. "Where do you want me to begin?"

He settles on the side of the desk, hands clasped on one thigh. "When did things start getting crazy, as you describe it?"

"That would be last week, when I had a phone call from a dead lady."

And I'm off, talking about Chrissy Burton and the identification mix-up, Bev Strait and her part in the transplant donations scheme, as well as about Jinx and Rex. I'm the one telling it, but it's as if I'm also listening, almost not believing my own words. It does, indeed, sound just this side of crazy.

"I'm wondering if this is more about something illegal going on with the whole donation for cash thing. I mean, I realize it's not illegal to sell things like plasma and bone marrow, but lobes from livers and lungs? I can't believe this is a good thing at all. I think you need to speak with Rex, since he's actually donated." I shrug, holding up my hands. "And I guess that's it."

Officer King reaches over and clicks the recorder off just as his partner sticks his head around the door.

"Hey, when you get a sec, come out back. I want to show you something." With a nod at me, he disappears back outside.

King lifts his backside off the desk and slips the recorder back into his pocket. "I'll get this report written up, and you'll be able to request a copy, if you'd like."

I thank him, assuring him I'm all right not having my own copy. "It's nothing I want to think about, believe you me." I think about Marta and what her reaction to this latest escapade will be, and I shudder inwardly. She is going to go bananas.

"Gij! Oh, my God! Are you all right?"

It's as if my very thoughts have caused her to materialize. Marta is here, flinging her arms around me and hugging me as tightly as she can.

Right behind her is Lou, a smug expression on her face. "I thought she ought to know as soon as possible, so I called her." Without another word, she heads back down the hall, whistling tunelessly under her breath.

"Which is more than you did," Marta says, staring at me with eyes as hard as obsidian chips. "When were you going to tell me? Over dinner? Before bed?"

Officer King slips out of the office with a half wave at me, a grin on his face. There's nothing like feeling abandoned by all and sundry. With a deep sigh, I draw Marta closer and begin to explain.

Once Marta is sufficiently calm, we head home, our vehicles making an impromptu parade. Both Lou and I have agreed to shutter the clinic for the remainder of the day, giving the staff a paid day off. Lou is taking the box of cats home for the night, more for distraction than anything else, I presume. It's been a trying day for all.

Marta goes to town in the kitchen, her remedy of choice when the world tips on its axis. It's definitely atilt at the moment. Being shot at has given me an unwanted glimpse of my own fragile mortality. I settle in at the kitchen table, watching her as she chops, stirs, and sautés her way to sanity. At least we'll both get a good meal out of this little episode.

I scrape up the last bit of stir-fried veggies and shrimp

and smile across the table. Marta has outdone herself, and I tell her so.

"I ought to come home early more often," I tease. Marta's eyes suddenly fill with tears. I shouldn't make light of things, but I can't help it. Gallows humor has always been my go-to reaction whenever faced with tragedy. "Sorry, love," I say with a grimace. "You know what I mean."

"It's not funny, Gij. All I kept thinking about was raising this little one without you around." She cradles her belly tenderly, and I swallow hard against the sudden lump in my throat. "I don't even want to imagine what that might be like, not even for a second."

A thought flashes into my mind, unwanted, unbidden. Maybe those who need a transplant feel the same? It makes the selling of organs seem much more sensible now for those financially able to skip to the front of the line. If it was me, I'd do anything to stay alive. Maybe even shoot at someone if I thought they were going to ruin my chance at a normal life.

"Do you think it was someone who'll lose out on a transplant if the whole scheme gets shut down?" I stare down at my plate, seeing Bev and Rex and Chrissy instead of dinner. "I mean, being killed outright is one thing, but it's got to be hard on a family to know death is waiting just a few years or even months down the road."

"I've seen you be altruistic before, Gij, but this is over the top, in my opinion. If I'd had a potshot taken at me, I'd be livid and wanting the one who did it caught." She takes another bite of food, effectively stopping the rest of her comments. I can see them in her eyes, though, and I know she's right. I should be hopping mad right now.

But I'm not. I truly want to know if this entire incident has anything to do with the donation plan, which will surely be shut down now. Instead of feeling triumphant, I feel like a heel. I wonder how many lives will be lost because of this, how many families will lose a loved one.

We get ready for bed silently, each wrapped in our own feelings. This is unusual for us. We typically use this time to talk about the day, rehash any issue that might have arisen or funny incident we might have witnessed.

My dreams are troubling, filled with someone bent on lassoing me with a rope made from dollar bills and intravenous tubing, tugging me toward the gaping mouth of an endless abyss.

CHAPTER TEN

Morning sickness has returned with a vengeance for Marta, laying her out flat on the bathroom floor. She doesn't even dare try to make it back to bed, and I bring her a pillow and several blankets, trying to make her comfortable, to erase the memory of last night. It's as if the baby has absorbed all of the angst from yesterday and is protesting.

"You need to get something in your stomach." I squat down next to Marta and push the hair back from her face. "Want some hot tea?"

"It'll just come straight back up," she says weakly, eyes still closed.

"Well, it's better than the alternative. I'll be right back." I know I sound pushy, but I'm not going to leave her lying here like this, dry-heaving her way to oblivion.

I have a feeling this will be an only child. No one in her right mind would be willing to go through this again. Of course, there's always Kate Middleton, I think wryly as I head downstairs. If a princess—or duchess or whatever she is—can soldier through this crap three times, and do it in heels…well, there's no telling what a mere mortal can do. And Marta Perry is no mere mortal.

I deliver the hot tea, and I'm pleasantly surprised to see she's made it to the bed. A childhood memory pops into my head and I create a pathway of towels from the bed to the bathroom. My sister and I used to joke that we always knew when someone had the stomach flu at our house because of the towel path. Our mom was a firm believer in forearming herself against childhood sickness, and she had a stockpile of home remedies and strategies we called "Mom 101." Who knew it would come in handy before the baby arrives?

I get ready to leave, assuring Marta I'll only be a text away. With the clinic closed for half a day yesterday, I predict we'll have a glut of appointments today. It's Murphy's Law, the one that says something about things going wrong if they can. Or is it awry? Whichever, it still means a busy day ahead of me.

"If you need anything, babe, anything at all, just text." I sit on the side of the bed, holding one of her thin hands in mine. This baby has become a little vampire, eating away at the essence that is Marta. "I'll keep my phone in my lab coat pocket. Promise."

"Thank you, my beautiful girlfriend, the most wonderful woman in the world," she replies. It actually comes out as "umm," but I'm adept at reading between the lines and the grunts. Smiling at my own silliness, I press a kiss on her forehead and head out to begin my day wrangling furry beasts.

The box full of cat and kittens is back in the reception area, placed under a hand-printed sign reading "Free to a good home." Of course, we'll offer to spay all the little ladies and neuter the gentleman free of charge as well. Mama Cat is already scheduled for her own snipping.

"How's Marta this morning?" Lou is sitting at her desk, flipping through a stack of invoices. That's her way of asking me if I'm still on Marta's bad list without making it obvious. I smile inwardly.

"Sick as a—Lou, why in the world do we always use dog

terminology for something bad?" I shake my head, feigning disgust at the verbal abuse canines take. "Sick as a dog. In the doghouse. Surly as an old dog. Why not cat? Or ferret?"

Lou lifts her massive shoulders, watching me from behind her reading glasses. She's already immersed in the paperwork lying in front of her. I sigh. I'm afraid it's a harbinger for things to come. Today is going to be a busy one.

I text Marta at different intervals, knowing she'll sleep through the soft trill of her phone's alert. If she answers, she's already awake. When I don't hear from her by three, however, I'm beginning to feel antsy.

After writing a script for an antibiotic and instructing the cat's owner on how to give it to him, I slip down the hall to the office. Following yesterday's bullet-ridden fiasco, I'll make my calls indoors, thank you very much.

"Come on, come on," I mutter into the cell phone, one hand jammed into my lab coat pocket. She's not answering, and when I get her perky voice mail message ("I'm either out having fun or busy planning some, so leave me a message!") I hang up in frustration. And fear. This is not like Marta. At all.

I leave the office, walking briskly from exam room to exam room until I find Lou. One look at my face, and she knows something is amiss.

"Is she all right?"

We've stepped into the hallway, just outside room two where a beagle pup is waiting to have its newly clipped tail looked at. Why owners persist on mutilating their animals is beyond me. Lou, I know, will be kinder than I would be.

"I have no idea," I say, forcing the words through tight lips. "She's not answering any texts, and it went to voice mail when I called."

"She could very well be sleeping, Giselle. When a woman is this sick, she needs all the rest she can get."

"Not for this long. Look at the time! It's already after three." I sound stubborn, but it's my way of worrying. Lou sighs. She can tell I won't be worth a plug nickel as long as I'm focused on Marta.

"Well, we've got it under control here. Why don't you take off, go check on her. And be sure to text me," she calls to my back. I'm already halfway out the door, anxious to get home.

Either I am completely lucky or the boys in blue are busy elsewhere, because I know I'm speeding to get home. I have convinced myself I'll find a disaster when I arrive, Marta completely incapacitated or worse. With a scrape of the tires against the curb, I pull up in front of our house and throw the Honda into gear.

I'm already calling her name when I hit the front steps, fumbling for my key. The door is unlocked, though, something we rarely do even when we're home, and my heart takes a flying leap against my ribs.

"Marta? Are you all right?" I stand in the hallway, listening intently to the silence, trying to hear movement of any kind. There is nothing. And now my heart is clambering to get out of my chest, beating like a timpani drum and threatening to burst. Something is definitely wrong.

"Gij? What are you doing home so early? Is everything okay?"

I'm not the fainting type, but I nearly fall over with relief when I hear her voice. Marta is peeking around the open front door, a curious Mr. Flores standing just behind her. Ignoring our neighbor, I grab her and hold her as tightly as I dare. The tears surprise both of us.

Later, sitting on the couch with Marta tucked securely in my arms, I am calm enough to listen.

"You know how technology hates me," says Marta, smiling

up at me. "Well, after I woke up, I wanted to text you to let you know I was feeling much better. Somehow, and I swear I have no idea how this happened, my charger got tangled up and wasn't working. And my phone was completely dead. I know how you worry, so I took a quick shower and went across the street to see if Mr. Flores had a charger I could use."

I can see fine lines around her eyes as she smiles. Mr. Flores is smiling as well, his small mouth pursed as he observes us. I want to tell him to go home, but Marta really likes him.

"So, did you ever get your phone charged?" I want these two to know how panicked I was, especially when she didn't answer my phone call. Maybe it's time to put in a landline. With a baby coming, it might be a good idea.

"That's the funny part," Marta says. She looks at Mr. Flores, and they both laugh.

There's a funny part to this?

"Yes," Mr. Flores says. "I didn't have a charger, and she couldn't remember your number. I offered her my house phone."

"I swear, being pregnant has sapped all my brain cells." Marta leans into me and plants a kiss on my cheek. "But everything is fine, and I'm glad you're home. Now, who's up for some coffee?"

Later, after I've extracted Mr. Flores from the chair and closed the front door firmly behind him, I discover I am beyond exhausted. Throwing myself down on the couch, I close my eyes and breathe in the lingering scent of Marta's perfume, Chloé by Lagerfeld, something I will always associate with her. If I were to walk in a room with my eyes closed and catch a whiff of that perfume, I would know she's there.

"Sorry I had you so worried." I open my eyes and see Marta kneeling beside me. "I honestly didn't think you'd be this upset."

I lift myself onto one elbow so I can look directly into her face. I'm tempted to play this out for all it's worth, but I can't. She looks too vulnerable, her eyes wide and hands resting on her belly, and I suddenly feel nothing but deep, protective love.

And I want to laugh.

"Marta, the two of us are such a pair of goofballs." I lean over and kiss her lips, swinging my legs around to sit up. "Here I am, worried about you, and here you are, worried about me. Who's left to worry about the kid here?" I lay one hand gently on hers, both of us hugging our baby.

"Mr. Flores?"

I just roll my eyes. But the emotional balance has been restored, and I pat the cushion beside me. We spend the rest of the evening cuddled together, talking about the future and making exaggerated plans we'll never fulfill. It's enough just to be here with Marta, here and alive and together.

Bless Lou's heart, I think when I arrive at the clinic the next morning. She not only took care of all the patients after I left, she also completed all the paperwork. When I find her leaning next to the coffeemaker in the break room, reading through today's appointments, I can't resist planting a huge kiss on her cheek.

"Hey, don't forget that you're already taken, woman." She makes as if to wipe off my kiss, but I can tell she's pleased.

"I can't resist a gal who gets it all done and still shows up the next day."

I reach around her and grab the coffee mug I keep at work. Marta bought it for me the last time we made the trek to the southern part of the state, visiting the happiest place on earth and acting like a pair of kids. I love it for a lot of reasons, but especially because it features Lady and the Tramp sharing their iconic spaghetti dinner.

We stand in companionable silence for a few minutes, waiting for the day to get started. Finally I sigh and push away from the counter. I can hear the chime ringing from the front door, announcing our first appointment.

"I guess I'll take the odds again," I say, giving Lou a smile over my shoulder. "Save you from dealing with the little guys today."

Our system is to put the smaller animals in the odd-numbered exam rooms, while the larger animals go into the evens. Lou prefers the bigger animals because she says they're much easier to handle. Of course, this doesn't always pan out, especially on days when every ferret, rabbit, and guinea pig in San Leandro finds their way to our clinic.

Today is one of those days. By noon, I've examined two kittens, an Angora rabbit, a ferret, and a pair of hamsters. Lou has had her hands full as well, including a visit with a puppy whose stomach was hard and distended. She's ingested a pacifier. The owner is upset, but Lou assures him she's seen worse. Surgery is scheduled for the next morning, and the puppy goes to our holding area where someone can keep an eye on her.

This reminds me of Rex and Tramp, and I wonder if the officers have spoken with him yet. I'm still thinking about this on my way home. As we eat dinner, I wonder aloud if there's a way I can find out if the San Leandro Police Department took me seriously.

"You could just call him," Marta says over a steaming bowl of jambalaya. I love it when she makes this, the pot brimming with shrimp, chicken, and sausage. It's a taste of New Orleans, one of our favorite cities in the whole world, the place we spent our first big weekend as a couple.

"I could," I admit, picking out a succulent shrimp and

popping it into my mouth. I've used my fingers, a habit that drives Marta wild, and I blow a kiss at her. "Maybe we should call Chrissy first."

"Why? What's she got to do with Rex?"

"Not a lot, but I still have a gut feeling she's the place to start." I fish another piece of shrimp out, staring thoughtfully down at my bowl. Something has jogged my memory, maybe a passing comment about being mixed up in the whole donation scene, or maybe it was it was just a suspicion I'd tucked away for later perusal. Whatever it is that's caused the thought, I still think Chrissy is the person to begin with.

"Speaking of fishing for info, have you heard anything from Don Butler? I'm dying to hear how his evening with Jinx went, aren't you?"

I'd completely forgotten about the fiasco that is Don Butler and Jinx. That's what getting shot at does for your memory, I guess. Between Marta's preggo brain fog and my memory loss, I don't hold out much hope for this baby of ours. Maybe she'll be adept enough to take care of herself. Her parents won't be much help.

"Maybe I should call Don first." I hesitate, thinking aloud, one hand hovering above my cell phone. I keep it beside me, but I leave it turned facedown so I'm not tempted to check for messages every few minutes. "He might have all the information we need."

"After an evening with Jinx? He probably knows more about Jinx and Rex than he bargained for." Marta laughs and nods at my empty bowl. "Want some more?"

"No, thanks. I think I'll pack some up for work tomorrow."

"Lucky you." She stands and reaches for my bowl. "Any time someone brings something with seafood in it, everyone acts like the plagues of Egypt have descended."

"Sissies." My attention is already on my phone as I thumb

through the list of numbers in my contacts list. Tapping on the phone icon, I settle back and wait for the call to connect.

"Don Butler. How can I help you?"

"Don, it's Giselle Cutler."

"Ah, just the woman I need to see. You got a minute?"

"To see or to talk?" His syntax has me confused. Does he want to come over here or just talk on the phone?

"Either. I'm leavin' this joint in about ten minutes."

"Hang on," I say, and then cover the mouthpiece with one hand. "Marta, would you mind if he swings by here? He says he needs to talk to us." I use an inclusive pronoun, hoping that this makes it easier for her to agree.

"No prob," she says promptly. "And tell him we've got plenty of leftovers if he hasn't had dinner yet."

I groan inwardly. The price I'm going to pay for this interruption of our evening is watching Don Butler eat tomorrow's lunch.

"Don, Marta says—"

"Yeah, yeah, I heard her. Tell her I'm starving. See you in a few."

And just like that, he disconnects. I hold my phone in the air, staring at it. "And here I thought people only hung up without saying goodbye in the movies."

CHAPTER ELEVEN

"That has got to be the best gumbo I've had in years," Don declares, leaning back in his chair and rubbing his stomach. "You lucked out in the kitchen department, Doc."

"It's jambalaya." I'm trying not to be irritated with his assumption that Marta is the kitchen magician. She is, of course, but I don't need my nose rubbed in it. "So, what did Jinx have to say?"

"Yes, do tell." Marta is leaning on her elbows, face alight with interest. "If he was half as entertaining as he was at the Vineyard, I can only imagine your evening."

"'Entertaining' is definitely the word for it." Don shakes his head, a half smile on his face. "Once I was able to drag him off the dance floor, he actually had some good information."

"You danced with him?" I can't resist teasing Don, knowing Jinx wouldn't need a partner to be the life of the party.

He shoots me a look that looks eerily like Marta's reaction whenever I've irked her. "No, I didn't dance with him. What I did was get a shitload of info that will curl your hair."

I raise my eyebrows, give him a nod. "So, spill it already. I'm assuming he told you stuff about the transplant hospital."

"And more." He looks across at Marta. "I don't suppose I could have any of that coffee."

"Of course," she says instantly, standing. I lean over and put a hand on her arm.

"You sit. I'll get super reporter here a cup."

"Hey, you wanna hear what he said or not?"

Don tries to sound offended, but I can see through it. He's posturing, trying on the alpha dog role and not quite getting it. I just give him the old shake-and-roll combo: shake my head and roll my eyes.

"We'd love to hear what you learned," Marta says with a smile for him and a frown for me. Oil on troubled waters, as usual. She is the appeaser, the mediator. "And if you've got room for dessert, I'm sure Gij won't mind getting you a slice of that strawberry cheese Danish we've got tucked away."

This time it's my turn to scowl. I'm watching my bedtime snack go the same way as my lunch. Chrissy Burton's peace of mind had better be worth the sacrifice.

"That really hits the spot," says Don. He leans back, wiping his mouth on the back of one hand. Out of the corner of my eye, I see Marta wince as she pushes the napkin holder across the table.

"Do you think you've got enough strength to talk, or do you need more coffee?" I let sarcasm leach into my words, my eyes on the now-empty Danish container.

"Give me a chance, Doc." He pushes back from the table, his gaze on Marta. "Can I use the can?"

"The can?" Marta is clearly confused.

"The bathroom," I say. "And you're not Ernest Hemingway, Butler." I look at Marta. "If he asks for a pipe and a cat, toss him out."

I can hear him chuckling as he heads to the guest bathroom. What a clown.

At Marta's suggestion, we've moved into the living room.

I start to protest, not wanting him to get comfortable. He's sitting in the same chair Mr. Flores favors whenever he visits.

I sit next to Marta, my arms crossed and my expression set. "So, what did Jinx the minx have to say?"

Don bursts out laughing, throwing his head back and giving us an unimpeded view of back teeth. "I like it," he finally says when he catches his breath. "Jinx the minx."

"Mr. Butler—"

"Don, please."

"Don, then." Marta gives him one of her lovely smiles, and it amuses me to see a faint blush on his cheeks. "Now, we're both dying to hear what you learned."

"After the dancing," I say. I get another jab in the ribs.

"Jinx and his brother are what you might call good-time Charlies, always on the lookout for the next adventure. The trouble is money. As you already know, Jinx works as a waiter. Rex works whenever the mood strikes him, which, according to Jinx, isn't very often. So, when Bev Strait came along with the perfect moneymaking scheme, well, there you go." He throws up his hands and lets them drop.

It's my turn to glare. "There you go *what*?"

Don shrugs, moving his shirt over bony shoulders. "That's it. It's just a way to get quick cash. It was Rex's turn this month, and next month it'll be Jinx's."

"Oh, hold on." I'm leaning rapidly toward irritation. If I gave up my leftovers and dessert for this crap, he'd better be quick on his feet. "I already knew this. What I want to know is what more Jinx said about Bev. What kind of business is she running from Rex's place? She's moved in there, in case you let *that* little tidbit slip your mind. And I'm still waiting for the curled hair you promised."

Another shrug. "She's a good woman, what can I say?"

"And you call yourself an investigative reporter." I don't even try to keep the disgust out of my voice. "We're done here, Mr. I-Think-I'm-Ernest-Hemingway." Standing, I point dramatically toward the front door. "Don't let it hit ya where the good Lord split ya."

Later, as we get ready for bed, I catch Marta smiling to herself as she watches me strip off my clothes and toss them in the corner.

"What?" I ask suspiciously, looking down at my naked body. "Is there something funny about the way I look?"

To my amazement, she lets herself sink down on the bed, sniggering helplessly as she holds her stomach. I wait out her fit of laughter with self-imposed stoicism.

"Oh, my God, Gij! I wish you could have seen your face when you sent him packing." She gives a gasp, trying to breathe through the laughter. "I haven't heard anyone say that little phrase since summer camp."

I have to grin, reaching for the oversized T-shirt I wear to bed. "Yeah, well, he was acting like an idiot, so I treated him like one." I jerk my head through the neckline, shoving my arms in the sleeves. "I think I'm pretty much done with him."

Marta rolls over on her back, crossing her arms behind her dark head. "I think he was having too good a time with Jinx and just didn't get to the investigation part of the evening."

I stop in mid-step as I walk toward the bathroom, my mouth hanging open. "No way. Do you think…" It's beyond me to articulate what I mean, but she gets me. Marta has been fluent in Giselle for quite a few years now.

"I have no clue, but did you see his face when you made that comment about dancing?" She giggles, a delightful sound I haven't heard much of lately. "He's either a late bloomer or a bad actor."

I snort. "I vote for bad actor. He can't even act like a reporter. And you know what? We probably know more about the whole situation than he does."

Marta is silent for a moment. Rolling on her side, which takes a little more effort than it did a few months ago, she asks, "Just what *is* the situation? Obviously, there's been a death, two personal attacks on you, an accident in the restaurant's parking lot, and something to do with organ donations. To me, that's four different issues."

I head for the bathroom as I debate her words. Gathering my hair back with an elastic band, I wash my face and brush my teeth, thinking about Marta's question. I've been seeing everything as connected, not separate. Is it possible I'm seeing ghosts when it's only my imagination?

Marta has moved to her side again. An odd expression is on her face, and she's holding her hand firmly on her belly. My heart races instantly, afraid for both Marta and the baby.

"Are you okay?" I kneel next to the bedside, my brows drawn together in concern. "Are you having pain?"

Her answer is to grab one of my hands and guide it to the same spot she's been touching. When I feel a gentle movement, my eyes grow wide and fill with tears.

"Is that..." I nod at my hand, unable to articulate my thoughts. Marta nods, her own eyes shining.

"I think so." She rolls on her back and pushes herself back onto the bed pillows. "I've been feeling it for a couple of days now."

She smiles at me, a tender expression on her face. She is the Madonna and Gaia in one. And she's going to be a perfect mom for our baby. Who knew a belly bump could make me so weak at the knees?

I'm still smiling the next morning as I navigate San Leandro's rush hour traffic. Marta, bless her heart, felt well enough to make a panini sandwich for me to take in place of the lunch lost to Don Butler.

"It's turkey, medium cheddar, and sliced apple," she said as she handed the small container to me. I wrinkled my nose. "Don't knock it until you've tried it. You need to eat more fruit, Gij."

"Isn't coffee a fruit?" I kissed her goodbye, ducking as she jokingly raised one hand. "Fine, I'll eat it. And thanks, babe. You make sure to eat today, too."

She rolled her eyes. "As if I need any encouragement. I woke up starving today, believe it or not. Do you think the worst is over?" She tilted her dark head to the side, her eyes inquisitive in the morning light.

"I could probably answer that better if you were of the canine or feline persuasion." I smiled as I got in another kiss, feeling her lips smiling back.

I carry that smile with me into the clinic. Lately, Lou and I have been toying with changing its name from the rather prosaic San Leandro Veterinarian Clinic to something a bit more catchy. Now that we've got a bullet hole in the back wall, maybe we should try something like the OK Pet Corral, except half the participants died at the original site. That might not send the desired message.

"Hey, Dr. Cutler," says a voice from down the hallway. "Can you come here a sec?"

It's Emily, our newest intern from the local college. She's serious at what she does, and she's usually waiting to be let in by whoever arrives first with keys.

That was me today, yet she's already inside. My heart picks up the pace as I walk briskly down the hall. I find her in the last exam room on the right, kneeling over a small bundle of fur on the table, its sides rising and falling in shallow gasps.

"I was afraid to move him," she says, trying hard not to

cry. "He was lying on the sidewalk in front of the clinic when I got here, and since the door was already unlocked, I just scooped him up and brought him in side." She looks up at me. "That's okay, right?"

"Absolutely," I say, setting my lips in a grim line. "Why don't you get the X-ray room prepped so we can see what's going on inside this little guy."

She dashes from the room, and I take her place, hovering over Tramp's small body and wondering how he ended up at my clinic. And why the front door was already open.

But first things first. I gently maneuver the Yorkie pup into my arms and walk as carefully as I can, not wanting to jar him any more than necessary. He doesn't make a sound, which can be both good and bad: good in that he's not in more pain and bad because he's not feeling pain as he should be.

Emily has switched the X-ray machine on and prepared a soft nest of towels on the table directly under the camera. I lay Tramp down on his side, and he feels unnervingly compliant. He should be wriggling, protesting at being left on a table. I exchange a glance with the intern, and I can see my own feelings mirrored on her face. We are both very worried.

I send Emily out of the room and follow her, taking with me the long, corded switch to activate the machine. I take a series of shots, carefully repositioning Tramp between each one, until I'm satisfied I've covered every inch of the small body. Whatever is wrong internally will show up on the finished X-rays.

"Well, looks like he's got severely bruised ribs and probably some damage to his liver, but he looks pretty good otherwise." I look from the lighted viewing box mounted on the wall to the table where Tramp is still lying, Emily standing nearby in case he starts moving. "Nothing looks wrong with his head, so I'm thinking this little guy is concussed."

As if on command, Tramp stirs and lifts his head with a slight whimper. Emily is instantly on hand, cradling the nest of towels and puppy in both of her arms. We both laugh when his soft pink tongue darts out and licks her nose.

"Hey, there, little guy." I bend over the puppy, gently stroking his fur. "I'm sure glad to see you awake." Looking up at Emily, I say, "Can you stay in here with him for a few minutes?"

"No prob, Doc," she says promptly and then blushes. "Sorry. I meant to say 'Dr. Cutler.'"

I grin at her as I straighten up. "'Doc' is fine, Emily. Makes me sound hip."

The expression on her face is priceless. "What's that?"

I grab at the lapels of my lab coat, feigning pain. "Ouch. And that tells me just how old I really am. Let's just say you can call me Doctor, Doc, or Goddess of Wisdom and Grace." I leave her puzzling over my words as I head to the front of the clinic.

Maxi is already at her desk, raven-black head bent over an iPad. She starts when I approach, and I can see dark circles under her eyes.

"You okay?" I'm solicitous of my staff, aware that happy and healthy employees mean a well-run office. "There're a lot of germs going around right now."

She shakes her head and smiles wryly. "I'm fine. It's self-inflicted, to be honest. I stayed up bingeing on Netflix until two. Gotta love *Stranger Things*."

Yikes. I can't imagine staying up that late, Netflix or not. "I see a nap in your future. Just not at the desk, all right?"

"Not even if I do it with my eyes open?" She's smiling, and I'm relieved to see her sense of humor is alert. "Oh, I found this on the desk when I got here." She lifts up the iPad and retrieves a small envelope from underneath. "It has your name on it, so I figure it's yours."

"Awesome deduction, Sherlock. Why don't you get a pot of coffee going? I sure could use some and you probably can as well."

The writing on the outside of the envelope is rounded, feminine. It's been done with some force, though, because I can see deep impressions in the paper when I tilt it sideways. Sliding a finger underneath the gummed flap, I draw out a single piece of folded paper and begin to read.

When I am finished, I am baffled. No, I am beyond baffled. Whoever wrote this note is either under the impression I am working with the police or I have some insider info on what's going on with Chrissy Burton. And she, if indeed the writer is a she, is not happy.

Withdraw yourself from the situation surrounding C. Burton or you'll be the next one lying in the street.

Lying in the street? As in Tramp? Or perhaps Bev Strait? This day is beginning to take on a surreal touch, and whether I like it or not, it's time to call the cops. Again.

CHAPTER TWELVE

The boys in blue have arrived, San Leandro's version of the cavalry. I'm both relieved and embarrassed to see a familiar face.

"This is getting to be a habit, Doc." Officer King, his expression both stern and amused, is standing just inside the front door to the clinic, a taller officer crowding in behind him.

I shrug, trying to appear nonchalant, and indicate a group of chairs in the reception area. "Would you like to sit here, or would it be better if we go to my office?"

"Here's fine." King glances behind him and jerks his chin at the other officer. "I'll talk with Dr. Cutler while you look at the front door. It was already unlocked when you arrived, correct?"

I nod. Behind the counter, I can see the wide eyes of Maxi as she listens to the conversation. I can only imagine what's going on in her mind. This clinic is beginning to resemble the Wild West. I groan inwardly, hoping I won't be looking for another receptionist before the day is done.

Officer King and I choose two chairs facing away from the door, him with his recorder balanced on his knee and me with a stomach in need of an antacid.

"When I arrived this morning, the front door was already unlocked. I honestly thought that Lou—that's Dr. Grafton—

had already arrived, and I came in without thinking anything about it."

"Do you recall seeing anyone hanging around outside, maybe watching you when you walked up?" The officer's eyes are the same shade of blue gray as his uniform, and I idly wonder if he chose this career to match his eyes.

And I need to have my head examined. Is this how people cross over from sanity to a proper crackup? Conscious of King observing me with those uniform-blue eyes, I flush. I'm sure I already appear crazy in his sight. I draw myself up straighter and rearrange my expression as I reply.

"No, unless you want to count that homeless guy who always stands under those trees across the street." I nod at the window as if I can still see him in his layers of old clothes, a worn Oakland A's cap covering his head.

"Ah. Steven." King nods as well, a small smile on his mouth. "You'd never know by looking at him he's got a doctorate in physics."

"Seriously? Are you sure?"

"Sure I'm sure. He used to teach at Berkeley back when I was in college." He shakes his head, but I see admiration there instead of sadness. "I never took one of his classes, but everyone said he was brilliant. I'll say this for him, he knows how to live."

I'm taken aback by this comment, but I offer no rebuttal. King might have a point, I think. Imagine not having responsibilities toward an employer or anyone else. The closer it gets to D-Day, Marta's due date, the more I can see the reasoning behind a disappearing act. Who knew I was such a coward?

"So, what about this note?" he asks. It's been placed inside an evidence bag King produced from his pocket, a magician in the forensic world. It's a good thing his frame is slender because he seems to carry the tools of the trade in his various pockets.

"The message is fairly straightforward, I would think. Shouldn't you be out there talking to Chrissy Burton?"

The corner of his mouth twitches slightly, the only visible reaction to my rather brash question.

"And why would I do that?"

I give a defeated shrug. "I don't know. Maybe because this is really about her and her situation. I really regret even letting that woman into my house, to tell you the truth."

Officer King sits in silence for a moment, eyes fixed on the small notebook resting on one thigh. Finally, he says, "I want you to think hard, Dr. Cutler." He lifts his head and stares straight into my eyes, and I can see something is troubling him. "When Ms. Burton first came to your house, what was your initial gut reaction?" I start to speak, and he holds up one hand. "No, I want you to take some time, really delve into your feelings. That's usually where the answers lie, in my experience."

My uneasiness is growing. This is taking on the tinge of a witch hunt, I think. No, not a witch hunt. More like a paranormal investigation. "Mrs. X, please tell us how you felt when you first walked into the house."

I shake my head, trying to dislodge these flights of fancy. Maybe I'm not sleeping enough. Maybe I'm a nutcase.

"To be honest," I begin slowly, "I was taken in by how upset she was when she showed up. It was like she'd been physically attacked or something. She really was a mess."

"Okay, let's start with that." King leans forward slightly, an intense expression in his eyes. "Did she say who was bothering her?"

I close my eyes, trying to recall the gist of our conversation that first day.

"From what I can recall, she was worried most about the mistaken identity of that woman they found in the bay. Apparently, the cops found something on her that made them think she was Chrissy, plus she looked enough like her to be a relative. But Chrissy said she was adopted and never knew her birth family."

"Has she been able to verify any relation to the dead woman? Done any type of DNA testing?"

"Yup. Marta and I both went with her to the lab." I give a half smile. "I have no idea what the results are, or if she's gotten them back yet."

"Well, that should be an easy fix." King closes the notebook and stands, smiling down at me. "I'll get an order of release."

"Wait," I say, standing as well. "Chrissy also said a DNA test probably won't clear anything up. She's a bone marrow recipient, which changes the individual's DNA makeup."

King folds his arms across his chest, feet spread wide. "That certainly muddies the water," he says dryly. "Any idea why she went ahead with the test?"

"No idea. That part has bothered me. Why would someone submit to a test they knew would be skewed?"

It's a rhetorical question. We're standing in silence when a series of sharp, high-pitched barks echoes down the hall. Tramp, I think. I'd almost forgotten about him.

"Officer, I completely forgot to mention the other part of this little problem." I nod toward the sound. "When Emily arrived this morning, she found one of our patients lying near the door, obviously in distress. The weird part is the puppy belongs to Rex, a bone marrow donor and a friend of Chrissy's personal assistant."

King's blue eyes twinkle down at me. "I was wondering when you'd remember to mention that part of the note."

I roll my eyes in self-deprecation. "Call it sympathetic preggo brain. The further along my partner is, the more I'm acting like her."

"It's a real thing," he agrees with a sardonic smile. "When my wife was expecting our first, I gained as much weight as she did. Of course, we had more money then, so I could actually buy lunch. Now it seems like every spare dime goes to the kids' activities." He shakes his head, but I can see he's happy. I sincerely hope I'll feel the same after little what's-it arrives.

With the typical request to call if I think of something else, the two officers leave. They've taken fingerprints and pictures and suggested we have the locks changed as soon as possible.

"I didn't see any signs of forced entry, so the perp had either a key or some sort of a burglar tool."

I bite my bottom lip, troubled at the officer's words. I'd like to think it was some type of jimmying tool, not an actual key. To me that smacks of someone lifting a key from one of our employees or an inside job. Either one is concerning, especially since no one has reported a missing key.

"Thanks. Another day, another issue, right?"

I meet Maxi's gaze. She quickly drops her eyes and begins shuffling and reshuffling a stack of invoices. I tuck this to the back of my mind for later perusal, curious if her reaction is voyeuristic or out of personal concern.

I make it through the day somehow, moving from patient to patient, administering vaccines and delivering diagnoses, checking in occasionally with Tramp. He is glued to Emily's side, both literally and figuratively. She's got him snuggled in a carry sack that hangs from the shoulders and tucks closely to her chest. His bright gaze moves from person to person as she goes about the day, only barking when he needs to be taken out back for a break. Rex has trained this puppy well.

Marta has arrived home before me, announcing her presence with an inviting aroma of cumin and chili. My guess is posole. Or white chicken chili. Either one is my favorite, I think with a smile as I dump my shoes and bag in the hallway.

"Honey, I'm home," I call out in my best Ralph Kramden impression. The only reply is the clatter of cooking utensils against stainless steel pots. Not quite the response I was hoping for. I peek around the doorway into the kitchen, a cautious cat assessing its territory for interlopers.

I spy one instantly. She is standing with her back to me, ramrod straight, one hand clutching a large ladle as if it's a lifeline. Or a weapon.

"Marta?" I walk into the room, hesitant at first. I know something has happened. I can feel it as if it were a tangible presence. "What's wrong, babe?"

"Chrissy Burton, that's what's wrong." She bangs the ladle down on the granite counter with so much force that I wince. "I want this to all go away, Gij." When she faces me, I can see her swollen eyes, her swollen belly. She's been crying.

Without another word, I'm across the kitchen with her in my arms, holding her as tightly as I dare.

"Can you leave the dinner for a few minutes?" I lean down and kiss the top of her head, nearly putting one eye out on an artistically gelled spike. "Let's sit down, all right?"

I guide her out of the kitchen into the living room. We are a two-headed, multilimbed beast, moving in harmony despite everything. I will keep it this way no matter what.

"So," I say into her hair as she sits encircled in my arms, "what happened?"

She reaches down to the front pocket of her maternity jeans and draws out a white envelope. I instantly recognize the writing on the outside and shudder. It's one thing to threaten me, but it's quite another when you come after my family. I take in a deep breath and read the note. It's a duplicate of the one I got.

"Where did you get this?" I sound sharper than I intend, but Marta knows me. It's my visceral reaction whenever I feel threatened or uncomfortable, and right now I'm feeling both.

"It was tucked under my windshield wipers when I left work." She cranes her neck and looks up at me, her dark eyes wide. "Gij, we've got to let this one go, let the police handle it. We can't afford to get involved in something this dangerous." She cradles her belly as if to reassure the baby that she'll protect it.

Swallowing hard, I put one hand on hers. If someone wants to bump heads with me, bring it on. Marta, however, doesn't see things this way and lets me know in no uncertain terms.

"Think about, it," I urge, striving to keep my voice even. "Chrissy Burton is the one who brought us into this whole mess. She needs our help, not our criticism." I draw in a breath through my nose and let it out through my mouth. Yoga breathing. Stress control.

"I'm not criticizing her, love. I'm just not sure we need to go any further with this. Let the SLPD handle it, okay? That's what they went to the academy for. You're a vet. I'm a social worker."

"And Chrissy's your boss." My neck muscles are beginning to tighten. I will them to relax, let my shoulders sag. It's a trick I've always used whenever I feel the fight-or-flight reaction beginning to appear. "Don't you feel some sort of loyalty to her?"

"Of course I do." Marta sounds hurt, and her body language is screaming contention loud and clear. Her arms are crossed high over her chest, fingers pressing into her skin.

I lean over and gently move her hands, holding them in

mine. I look down and can see the half-moon impressions left by her nails, a sure indication she is heading toward anger.

"Love, I'm not disagreeing with you, I'm really not." I gently kiss the side of her head. "And I get why you want to be done with this, but I still think I need to see this through. I owe it to Chrissy."

Marta begins to laugh, a slightly hysterical sound that troubles me. Since the beginning of the pregnancy, her emotions have roller-coastered all over the place, but this is a new one on me. I hope I don't have to fall back on the time-honored response to hysteria. If I have to slap Marta, she'll probably slug me back and move me to the guest room permanently.

Finally she gasps, wipes her eyes, and plants a kiss on my cheek.

"That was the best laugh I've had in a while," she says, her eyes bright and cheeks pink. "And don't ask me why I think that's so funny, but I do. Giselle Cutler, knight in shining armor." And she's off again, giggling madly and clutching her stomach. If nothing else, our baby is getting a good workout.

I don't know whether to be flattered or irritated. I decide on hungry.

"Hey, you." I give Marta's shoulders a little shake and stand up. "I don't know about you, but I'm starving. Want me to bring you dinner in here?"

She wipes her eyes on the corner of the voluminous top she's wearing and holds out one hand to me. I lift her to her feet and give her a gentle hug.

"No, I want to eat at the table. I'll probably be couch-bound soon enough." She grins up at me, her dimple winking from the corner of her mouth. "Just think, Gij. Pretty soon you'll be the one making dinner for me."

I shudder, not bothering to hide my reaction. Despite

my wish that this pregnancy be over soon, I'm dreading the inevitable.

Time to start collecting takeout menus.

We spend a quiet evening in front of the television, catching up on *Stranger Things* and trying to second-guess the season's ending. It's nice, I think, to sit here with Marta, relaxed and safe.

Except we're really not. Whoever left us the twin notes knows who we are and how we're connected. They probably already know where we live, and certainly know where we both work.

When the show is over and Marta has gone upstairs, I walk the house twice, double-checking windows and outside doors, making sure we are locked in securely for the night. I don't know who is watching us, stalking us, threatening us. Whoever it is, though, had better watch out. Reaching into the downstairs closet, I retrieve my metal softball bat and carry it with me to the bedroom, keeping it within arm's reach.

My last thought is that maybe I should come with the warning that I batted .750 last season. I rarely miss.

Chapter Thirteen

When the morning comes, I'm both relieved and irritated I did not have a chance to show off my batting skills. Marta, on the other hand, is beyond glad. She thinks I would have probably hit a wall instead of the intended target.

"We need to concentrate on getting a nursery ready, Gij, not on fixing holes in walls." She smiles at me from the bathroom doorway, and I can see an imprint from the sheets on one cheek. Her color is good this morning, rosy instead of the wan complexion that has been typical of the past few months.

"Just get that honey-do list ready, and I'll get on it," I say as I lean down to fasten the Velcro straps of my running shoes. My plan is to get some exercise in before I hit the shower, something I haven't done in a while. Hopefully, I won't pull a hammie and have to call Marta for a lift home.

Marta tosses her head as she heads for the stairs.

"What?" I call out after her, trying to sound offended. "Don't you believe me?"

"Nope." Her one-word answer floats back up the stairs and I grin. She knows me too well.

"Yeah, well, guess I'll have to prove you wrong." I run down the stairs and stop in the kitchen to grab a bottle of water and a kiss before I take off. "You write the list, I'll get it done."

The morning air is damp, the fog rolling around like something live and wild. Carl Sandberg's famous cat would be a tiger here in the Bay Area.

I can't even see the end of our street from the front yard, but my view of Mr. Flores's house is clear as a bell. I can see him moving around his kitchen, walking slower than he does when in public. Hopefully he isn't getting ill, I think. Marta will feel obligated to play nurse, something I don't think she needs to do at the moment.

It's good to feel the movement as I start jogging, running easily along the sidewalk snaking around our block. Since returning from our ill-fated trip to Arizona, I've taken up sporadic exercising. It's a good way to banish negative feelings and has actually improved my sleeping patterns—when Marta isn't snoring, that is. Thankfully this is something that's cleared up slightly since her pregnancy. She's sleeping more on her side these days instead of on her back, and her typical starfish pose has morphed into something compact, more protective of her belly. Even in her sleep, Marta is a fierce mama bear.

When I hit the end of the block I hesitate briefly, jogging in place, trying to decide whether or not to turn and complete the circuit or to keep going straight. The fog in this portion of the street is thicker, swirling in front of me as I pound the pavement.

The roar of a motor startles me, causing me to stutter step and nearly fall into the street. As the metal grille of the SUV materializes out of the fog and heads straight for me, I catch my shoe on a hillock of grass edging the sidewalk and tumble sideways, knocking my shoulder hard against a fire hydrant. I lie there for a moment, a turtle on its back, as the vehicle squeals its tires and heads back into the fog.

How it misses me is a wonder. Or a miracle. Or bad driving.

Later, Marta points out my moment of indecision is probably what saved me from being injured or even killed. She may be right, of course, but I tend to compartmentalize, so this is one memory I've revised and tucked away.

I get back to my feet and make a feeble attempt to brush away the grass stains on my knees. Marta will see it right away, I know, so I debate sneaking back into the house and into the shower.

"Doctor C, are you okay?"

I look over my shoulder and spot Mr. Flores across the street, standing with his hands on his hips as he cranes his neck to see through the mist. Nodding, I try to brush off the incident along with the grass, convincing myself it was an accident, a distracted driver.

"I was just startled and managed to trip myself up, that's all." I force a layer of jollity over my words and begin walking back toward my house, trying not to limp. "Guess I'd better get home and cleaned up before Marta spots this. She'll be teasing me about this forever if she does."

"I think it was aiming at you."

His words give wings to the thoughts fluttering inside my head like birds trying to escape from a trap. I give a short laugh.

"Nah, probably just someone trying to text and drive. No one thinks the laws are meant for them, right?"

Mr. Flores follows me home from his side of the street, keeping pace with me as I try to walk without appearing hurt. When I reach the front of the house, I give him a jaunty wave and head inside, careful to close the door quietly behind me.

"Just can't take you anywhere, can I?" Marta's gaze is fixed on my green knees. "Looks like someone needs training wheels just to walk."

"You know me, grace personified," I say, hoping she'll

leave it at that. "I'll get cleaned up and then head out to work. You leaving soon?"

Wrong question. I've just cracked open the door to her curiosity. She's got intuition in spades.

"Any reason why Mr. Flores felt the need to shadow you home?" She puts her hands on her hips, head cocked to the side, eyes fixed on my knees. "Anything you need to tell me, Gij?"

"Moi?" I aim for flippant and encounter a brick wall of silence. Sighing, I slump down on the bottom step, hands clasped loosely between my telltale knees. "Fine. I just missed getting hit by a truck."

Marta's screech is loud enough to be heard in downtown San Francisco.

When I've finally talked her down from the emotional ledge she's standing on and have assured her I am all right, apart from bruised knees and equally battered ego, I make my way up to the shower. I turn the water as hot as I can stand it—"lobster style," Marta likes to call it—and rotate my neck under the water. I'm beginning to ache all over now, feeling the tension from my neck down to my toes.

"Still think it was an accident?"

I start as Marta thrusts her face into the shower, breaking into my reverie.

"You're going to give me a heart attack," I say, striving for playful as I hold out one hand. "Wanna join me?"

"No, I don't want to join you." She draws back slightly, and I can see water droplets on her skin. "What I want is for you to join *me*, Gij. I want you to talk to me, be honest with me." She places one hand on her belly almost unconsciously, and something akin to anger blooms in my chest. How dare she play the holy mother, the perfect mother, with me? I'm as invested in this as she is.

It must have made its way from my chest to my eyes, because she stares at me in horror and stumbles away from the shower, leaving the room and me as well.

This is territory neither of us has ever visited before.

This is not going to happen in my life.

I slam the water off and grab a towel, not bothering to drape it fully around my body before I charge out of the bathroom and head for our room.

"Marta, wait." I catch her just as she's heading down the stairs. Her dark head is bent so far over, I'm afraid she'll miss a step and tumble to the bottom. "Marta, stop. Please."

Thankfully she does, pausing below me on one riser, one hand on the banister and the other held over her mouth. I stop on the stair just above her and place a tentative hand on her shoulder.

"Please," I say more softly. "Please don't leave like this. This just isn't us, love."

She takes her hand away from her mouth, but her head remains bowed. This breaks my heart more than anything else. Marta is not given to folding in on herself, either literally or figuratively.

"Gij, I can't do this anymore."

For one moment, my heart feels as though it has imploded. If I lose Marta, I lose myself.

She turns her head and looks directly at me, and I can see her eyes are red-rimmed and puffy. My imploding heart breaks.

"Come here," I say in a voice as unsteady as my breathing. I hold out one hand to her as I sink down on the staircase. Below us the grandfather clock strikes the hour, reminding me both of us have places to be. I could not care less.

She takes my hand and allows herself to be helped back up. I put one arm around her and pull her close, fighting down an urge to hold on as tightly as I can. I want to give her room to breathe. I want to give her room to leave. I want to hold on forever.

We sit in silence for a few minutes, the only sound the gentle ticking of the grandfather clock's pendulum. Finally, Marta gives a shudder, reminding me of a child whose sobbing has quieted in its mother's arms. I feel my own eyes welling with tears, and I swallow hard, tightening my jaw in an effort to hold them back. My chipmunk face. The one that tells others I'm keeping everything at bay.

"Marta," I say as I take in a careful breath, "I love you more than I've ever loved anyone. Whatever is going on, we can get through it. Together."

"You're scaring me, Gij," she whispers so softly I have to lean over to hear her words. "I don't like what's happening to you."

Her words take me aback, and I have to process them before I can even begin to unravel any meaning. What *is* happening to me? I am still a hardworking woman, a veterinarian who loves her job, someone lucky enough to have a partner who gets me and who loves me. What has changed?

Marta, as though reading my thoughts, clarifies them for me.

"In my opinion," she begins hesitantly, "the more dangerous this entire situation gets, the more flippant you are. It's like, I don't know, a midlife crisis of sorts." I start to protest but she hushes me with a finger placed gently on my lips. "See it from my perspective, Gij. We're going to be parents in just a few short months, and I want you to be around to do some of the parenting, all right?"

I want to defend myself against her words, but I can't. I don't know if I agree with her assessment that this is a midlife crisis. Am I old enough for one of those? But I can see her point. I have become reckless, brushing off danger without letting it settle on my shoulders. Is this how soldiers feel after they've survived battle and bombardment? Is it possible I'm experiencing some form of post-traumatic stress? Being shot at is no walk in the park, believe me, but I acknowledge it has made other situations seem less than they probably are.

"I'm sorry," I say, having no other words at the moment. "I'm so sorry, love."

And I begin to cry.

Marta somehow gets both of us to our feet and back upstairs. She guides me toward our bed and I lie down, conscious my body has air-dried and my hair is beginning to curl up around my face. When she draws the comforter up over my shoulders and tucks it in around me, I am suddenly four again, a little girl whose mother is there, running cool fingers through my hair and softly humming a tune under her breath. I drop off to sleep without another thought.

Sometimes, a crossroads presents itself in terms so obvious that disregarding it is ignorant. By the time I hear Marta's tread on the stairs once more, I have determined to reassess my involvement in the Chrissy Burton case.

"How're you feeling?" She perches on the side of the bed and smooths the tangled curls away from my face. "You must have been exhausted. You've been in bed since I left for work."

I stretch my arms above my head and reach toward to the end of the bed with my toes, enjoying the movement of limbs that have been still all day.

"I think I've been mentally tired, love." I prop myself up on one elbow and rub a hand over my face as I yawn loudly. "Hope I can sleep again tonight."

"Sounds like you won't have any problem in that department. Why don't you grab a rinse off while I throw some dinner together, all right?"

I pretend to consider this suggestion, putting one hand to my chin in my best Rodin pose. When Marta reaches out to ruffle my hair, I trap her hand against my cheek and turn my head to kiss her palm.

"Thanks, love," I say.

I put a lot of meaning behind those two words: I love you. Thanks for putting up with me. I'm sorry.

Marta knows what I mean even when I don't say it. With a quick kiss on my forehead, she stands up from the side of the bed and her shirt catches in the waistband of her pants, exposing part of her belly. For one crazy moment, I think I see movement there and my breath catches. She looks at me and grins.

"Did you see that?" Placing both hands on her middle, she laughs down at me and shakes her head. "This kid is either going to play soccer or be a ballerina."

Dinner is easy, and I don't just mean the menu. I can feel a softness between us that hasn't been there in a while. I am determined to keep it going for as long as I can, even if it means getting serious about safety at the clinic. I mean, I'm already safety conscious, and so is Lou. But if backing out of the whole Chrissy Burton mystery will keep my family safe, then so be it.

I'll leave the crime solving to the good guys and gals in blue.

CHAPTER FOURTEEN

I like to think I follow advice with an open mind and a willing heart, even when the advice comes from me. That might place it in the category of Jiminy Cricket, of course, as in letting my conscience be my guide. Marta probably has a more realistic view of my abilities in this area, though, so she merely rolls her eyes when I announce my intentions after dinner to give up my fledgling crime-fighting career.

"Until the next big thing comes along," she says as she moves a cushion behind her back and grimaces.

"What's wrong?" I kneel down beside the couch, concerned something has gone wrong with the baby.

"Nothing. Just growing pains. They're only beginning, I'm afraid."

This whole pregnancy thing is more complicated than I had imagined it would be. And just think, there's another two trimesters to go. Yippee.

I move over to an armchair and let my body conform to its cushioned lines. "I think I'm having sympathy pains," I say, putting one hand on a hip and giving my back a twist. "Back to what you were saying."

"Or you were in bed too long." Marta's smile takes the sting out of her words.

I have to agree. Even my teenaged self would have had a tough time sleeping all night and then all day. I give my back a final rub and then nod across the room at Marta. "Go ahead. I'm all ears."

She stares at me for a moment and then transfers her glance to the ceiling, crossing both arms behind her head. Her posture reminds me of someone on a psychiatrist's couch, ready to spill their innermost thoughts. I hope I'm ready for this.

"Gij, from the time I met you, I've always known you to be a ready-fire-aim type of person. That's not necessarily a bad thing," she says over my feeble protests. "I figured as long as I could head whatever was bothering you off at the pass, so to speak, I could help you."

Half-buried memories begin to surface: Marta playing the peacemaker between me and my sister before Leif was born. Marta offering to handle situations and people I found irritating. I give a tiny shrug in agreement.

"What I need from you now, Gij, is for you to focus on us." Marta gently strokes her belly as she smiles over at me. "I'm thankful you're such a knight in shining armor, I really am, but not when your life is at stake." She gives a short laugh. "And I know that sounded dreadfully melodramatic, but I mean it."

I swallow hard against the treacherous knot in my throat. Marta's words have touched me.

"I really meant what I said," I say, sitting forward with my elbows on my knees and my hands clasped. "I do have one thing I need to take care of first, though, and I swear that'll be it. All right?"

I fully expect Marta to throw up her hands in response. Instead, she continues to look across at me with her dark eyes, eyes whose depths are so murky I can't read her thoughts. I can imagine them, though, and they aren't pretty.

"Fine," she says as she twists over on her side. She punches the pillow down with such ferocity that I wince. "You do that, whatever it is. But I swear on a stack of Val McDermid books, Gij, this better be it." Those last words are snapped off as cleanly as flint. I almost salute at their sound.

"Cross my heart and hope to die, stick a needle in my eye," I solemnly intone, my expression as sincere as I can manage just before I burst into laughter. "Really? A stack of Val McDermid books?" I shake my head in amusement as I get to my feet. "Only you, Marta. Only you."

"Whatever it takes." She holds out one hand, and I walk over to take it in mine, bending down to kiss each slender finger one by one. "And I don't know about you, but I can hear my side of the bed practically yelling at me to get my hiney in gear and get up there."

I pause and cup one hand behind my ear, pretending to listen intently.

"That's funny. All I can hear is that pint of Chunky Monkey ice cream in the freezer calling my name."

"Whatever." Marta swings her feet over the edge of the couch and stands in one fluid motion, quite an accomplishment for someone whose lap is rapidly disappearing. "Go get your ice cream. I'll meet you upstairs. And bring two spoons."

This time I do salute. Marta gives me a silent one-fingered wave that makes me smile. She still has that sass I've always liked, and I can only imagine what our child will be like. Hopefully she or he will like ice cream as much as I do and be as spunky as Marta.

I fall asleep around midnight, long after Marta has begun her snore-and-whistle combo. My last thought is that I need to get hold of Don Butler.

Lou is in a mood the next morning, responding only in

grunts and scowls to my conversational overtures. Finally, I've had enough and stomp out of the office toward the reception area, nearly falling over the clinic's adopted cat mama and her gaggle of kittens. I catch myself on the edge of the counter but hit my injured knee against the sharp edge of an end table that seems in cahoots with the kittens.

"Damn it!" I grab at my knee with both hands, holding it as a new trickle of blood begins to ooze through the thin material of my work scrubs.

"Are you okay, Dr. Cutler?"

I look up and see Maxi peering over the top of the counter, suddenly recognizing her eyes from somewhere besides the clinic. And it clicks.

"You're Jinx's sister, aren't you?"

"And Rex's as well," she says, giving a wry smile. "So, yeah, I recognized Tramp, before you ask. I'm so glad he'll be okay."

"Hold up." I shake my head as I attempt to make all the pieces fit. "So, if Rex is your brother, and you recognized Tramp, are you saying you know he left the letter? Rex, I mean, not the dog."

She has the grace to look embarrassed. "He might have mentioned someone gave him the note to pass on to you."

"Did he say who it was?" I'm beginning to suspect I already know the answer.

"No," she says emphatically. "He told me it would be better if I didn't know who it was."

Fabulous. There goes one possible link to the Chrissy Burton issue. Her next words, however, stop me cold and leave me feeling much the same way.

"I tried to get hold of him to tell him Tramp was all right, but he's not answering his phone. And he's not at his apartment either." Tears fill her eyes and threaten to spill over. "And Jinx hasn't heard from him either."

She also could have mentioned her connection to Jinx that day he visited the clinic, but I decide to let that dog stay asleep. First things first. I need to find Rex, if only to give him a piece of my mind for playing these idiotic games.

"When was the last time you tried to get in touch?" My knee is still smarting and is probably still bleeding, but I ignore it. I'll have to change before I see any patients today, obviously, but for now I'm focused on this new crisis.

"Just before I came to work." She swallows hard against the tears, staying in control. I admire that, especially since I've been described as leaning toward the non-emotional end of the spectrum. Some of us prefer to react in private. Not everyone turns into a public puddle when drama hits the fan.

"Right." I hobble over to the counter, favoring my sore leg. "Is there anyone you can call in to cover your shift today?"

The change of topic takes her aback for a second and then she nods.

"Sure. I can call Akemi. She volunteers at the animal shelter sometimes, and she also does some temp work."

"Okay, take care of that. I'm going to let Dr. Grafton know you and I are going to be gone for a while this morning." Without another word, I turn and limp back down the hallway, narrowly missing an errant kitten that seems intent on tripping me up.

I meet Lou as she comes out of the supply room, juggling an armful of disposable glove and tissue boxes. It's allergy season in our part of the state, and it seems as though we go through more tissue lately than we do anything else.

"Hey, I need to take off for a while. Maxi's going with me and she's calling someone named Akemi to cover the desk and phones." I reach out to steady the pyramid of boxes in Lou's arms. Lou looks pointedly at my leg.

"Been wrestling gators lately?"

I give a short laugh. "Nope. Just being my typically clumsy self." I look at her closely, trying to judge her mood. "I thought Marta might have mentioned it yesterday when she called me in."

"If she did, I didn't hear about it."

Ah. Maybe Marta didn't call in for me after all. No wonder Lou's snapping sparks at me this morning.

"Long story short," I begin, leaning over to pull up my uniform's pant leg, "I went for a run and almost got run over myself."

Lou squints and leans in closer, losing the top two boxes of tissues from her already tottering stack. Without thinking, I bend down to retrieve them. When our heads hit, it's as if fireworks have gone off behind my eyes.

"If we're not careful, we'll both be limping out of here." Lou frees one hand to rub her forehead, sending the rest of the tissue boxes tumbling to the floor.

This time neither one of us makes a move. It's broken the ice between us, though, and we exchange conspiratorial grins.

"Maxi!"

We call her in concert, a wide-eyed Maxi peering around the corner of the front desk and cautiously joining us.

"Would you help me get these things put in the exam rooms?" Lou nods at the tissue, gingerly squatting down to begin picking them up. Her knees give a twenty-one-gun salute, popping with enough noise to rival even my bad joints.

"Sure, Dr. G." With the grace of the young, Maxi bends over and begins gathering the boxes, stacking them neatly in the crook of one arm. "And I just got off the phone with Akemi. She'll be here in the next twenty minutes, she says."

"Awesome." I watch as Lou heads to the nearest exam room. "Let's be ready to go as soon as she gets here, all right? It might be a good idea to make her a list of everything she'll need to know."

And it will give me a chance to dash off an email to Don Butler. Without another word, Maxi heads off to deliver the tissues. I walk to my office, already composing the email in my mind.

Of course, it might be easier and more expedient to send him a text. Slumping back in my desk chair, legs stretched out to avoid bending my sore knee, I thumb through my recent phone calls.

I need to see you ASAP. Available this morning? I tap out the message using one finger.

He answers my text almost immediately. *Am driving. Will respond later.*

Damn. I love our state's no texting while driving law, I really do, but sometimes it can be just this side of irritating. There's nothing to do but call him. Hopefully he's on hands-free.

He answers after two short rings.

"Don Butler here." I can tell by his slightly muffled tone that he is on a hands-free device, but he's eating. Isn't that just as dangerous as using a cell phone?

"It's Giselle." Close your mouth, I want to say. "I need to talk to you as soon as you're free."

"Funny," he replies. I can hear the sound of paper rustling in the background. A breakfast burrito wrapper, or maybe one from an egg sandwich. "I was just on my way to see you. You know what they say about great minds and all that jazz."

"Well, this great mind wants to run a few things past you. Where are you right now?"

"Just pulling into the parking lot behind your clinic."

"Fabulous." I stand up quickly, forgetting about my knee and whacking it soundly on the edge of the desk. "Ow!"

"Hey, it's not that painful to talk to me."

"No, it's something else." I press my lips tightly together in an effort to mitigate the pain, or at least my reaction to the pain. "Come around to the front door, all right?"

By the time he arrives, I've hobbled down the hallway into the reception area.

"Thanks for coming by," I say, forgetting he was already on his way here. I glance over to the front desk where Maxi is writing the note, her bottom lip between her teeth. "We're just waiting for the replacement receptionist, and we can go somewhere else to chat."

Don stares at me but he says nothing, instead doing a one-eighty as he looks around at the office.

"Nice digs. And who's this cutie?" He bends down, ready to scoop up a kitten that's wandered close, swiping one tentative paw at his shoe. Mama cat is hovering just in the background, though, and he wisely limits the contact to a brief tickle between the kitten's ears.

"Smart move," I say, a lopsided grin on my face. "That's one of a new batch we're trying to find homes for. Interested?"

"Maybe," he says, much to my surprise. I'd been half joking. "Speaking of homes, I got a tip about Jinx's brother. Something about his home being ransacked."

A slight sound comes from the desk, and I look over in time to see Maxi slide from the chair onto the floor.

"Was it something I said?" Don stares at the fallen girl as I limp in double-time to the desk and check to make sure she's still breathing. I'm relieved to see she's landed on a large cushion meant for the kittens, and her eyes are already opening.

"It's a long story. And after you've gotten her a drink of water, I'll tell it you."

Without another word, Don bolts down the hallway. I have to admit the man can move for someone his age.

CHAPTER FIFTEEN

With Maxi now leaning back against the cushions of the love seat, I relax. I don't think I've ever actually seen someone faint when hearing bad news, and I am relieved to see her color has returned. Don, on the other hand, is looking more than a little guilty at having caused the episode. Maybe I can play on that and get more information than I have to give up.

The front door opens, and a slight young woman walks in. She starts to smile when she spots Maxi, a pair of dimples deep enough to hold water standing out on either side of her mouth.

"Hey, girlfriend," she says, tossing a macramé bag on the floor and sinking down next to Maxi. "You sick or something?"

I jump in before Maxi or Don say anything. "Something. Are you good for the rest of her shift?"

"Sure thing." She shrugs her thin shoulders, reaching up to tuck a length of shining black hair behind one ear. "I've gotta study for midterms, if that's okay. The profs at Berkeley could care less how busy my life is." This is directed at me and I nod, vaguely sympathetic. I'm not so old I can't recall my own frustration at the mountains of work my teachers seemed to invent from thin air.

"No problem, as long as it's quiet here. I'm sure you know how busy a clinic can get at the drop of a hat."

"You're telling me," she says, rolling her dark eyes. "I swear, sometimes it seems like every dog and cat in the Bay Area gets sick on the same day, you know?"

I did indeed know. Toss in a few ferrets and pets of the smaller variety, and you'd have a real humdinger of a day. A twinge of guilt shoots through me. No wonder Lou's ticked off, having to fly solo so often lately.

"Maxi, you ready?" I reach over and pat the girl's arm. She nods, moving to the edge of the seat and standing up, swaying slightly. Akemi and I grab for her at the same time, steadying her as she stands still, eyes closed.

"Maybe we should postpone this," Don offers, an uncomfortable expression on his face. "I mean, we can talk later if she's not feeling well." He gives a surreptitious glance at his watch. "I can always meet you later, Doc."

"I'm fine." Maxi's voice is firmer than I would have expected for someone who's just fainted, but what would I know? I've never passed out in my life.

I glance from Maxi to Don, aware of Akemi's bright gaze flitting between the three of us. We need to take this somewhere else, or we'll become fodder for dormitory gossip.

"Don, do you want to drive? Or I can, if you want me to." I glance down at my leg and see the blood on my scrubs has dried. I hesitate a moment, trying to decide whether or not to change before I go out in public. Marta's voice in my head wins out, and I excuse myself to put on a clean pair of bottoms. "Just give me a sec, okay?"

Finally we're in Don's van, and I have to use the sole of one shoe to push the debris on the floorboard to one side.

"Eat fast food much?" I ask dryly.

"You should see what's back here," says Maxi, something like awe in her tone. I can hear the crinkle of paper moving around on the back floorboard. "I haven't seen this franchise for at least five years." She holds a hamburger wrapper up for us to see.

"Oh, hardee har har, very funny." Don doesn't sound upset, though, and it occurs to me he might see the various strata of trash as a testament to how hard he works, how busy his life is. I just shake my head, imagining Marta's reaction. "So, where do you two want to go?"

My phone buzzes against my hip, and I know it's Marta. We often have this seemingly psychic connection. I think of her and she calls, and vice versa.

"What's up, buttercup?" she says in my ear, and I'm thrown off my conversational stride.

"You called me," I say, giving a small shrug at Don's quizzical glance. "What's up with you?"

"Well, since I just left the clinic and was told by someone I don't know that you'd left with Maxi and a strange man, I think you're the one who needs to answer that question."

I grin as I glance sideways at Don. He is a strange character, but I seem to collect these by the handful. "Wanna join us?"

"Absolutely," she says without hesitation. "Where are you going? I can take an Uber and meet you there."

"Hang on a sec," I say, then turn to Don. "Marta wants to meet up with us. Where should I tell her to meet us?"

"Could we go by Rex's apartment first?" Maxi leans forward, poking her face between the two front seats.

He shrugs as he maneuvers the van into traffic, narrowly missing a parked car and getting a cacophony of horns in return.

"Fine by me," he says as he leans on his own horn in response. The ooga noise catches me by surprise and makes me laugh aloud. He grins and punches the horn again. "Like that, huh?"

"I love it!" Maxi and I say in unison, and we laugh. She seems to be feeling much better, thank goodness. I'm getting to be quite the Florence Nightingale with Marta, but I'm not too sure how I'd do with someone else. My maternal gene still seems to be on the blink.

"So, Maxi, what's the quickest way to get there?" Don asks. "I can use GPS, but I figure you'll know the back way."

"No problem," she assures him. Scooting forward on the seat, she points to the next street. "Take a right here, then a left."

"What the heck is all that noise?" Marta says, her words underpinned with anxiety.

"Just Don's driving," I say. "We're headed to Rex's apartment, so you can meet us there." I give her the directions and we disconnect. I'm suddenly feeling a bit more cheerful, knowing Marta will be there.

We arrive in front of Rex's apartment complex in record time. It's a multiple-story concrete building, but what might have been an austere edifice is soft, with fanciful swoops and curves across the Spanish tile roofline and along each wall. And it's very familiar to me, as if I've been there before. Marta is already there, and we exchange a brief kiss before turning back to the building.

Maxi catches my curious expression as I stare up at the building and laughs.

"Do you recognize it? Most folks do, at least those who are die-hard Alfred Hitchcock fans."

"It's from *Vertigo*," I say with a grin. My parents looked

down their noses at television. We never had one in the house, but they loved old films. Our local library had a weekly movie night on a monthly theme, so one glorious summer month we were introduced to *The Birds*, *Vertigo*, *Rear Window*, and *Notorious*.

"Not bad, not bad." Marta pats my arm. "How did I not know I'm living with a trivia genius?"

Walking ahead of us next to Maxi, Don turns and gives us the benefit of his rather sharklike smile. "Don't tell her that. She's bigheaded enough as it is."

"Takes one to know one."

"Okay, children, let's play nicely." Marta, always the peacemaker, reaches over to slip an arm around my waist. "Let's remember why we're here, all right?"

She couldn't have chosen colder words to toss over the exchange, bringing the emotional temperature down to near freezing. The four of us walk soberly into the building, its insulated silence underscoring the mood. It feels as though we've walked into a setting, a stage for something that will impact all of us. I shiver slightly, and Marta tightens her arm around me.

And when we arrive at the door of Rex's apartment, that feeling intensifies.

Don, who is surprisingly silent, motions for Maxi to announce our presence. She knocks on the door tentatively at first, then harder. There is no answer, of course. I didn't expect there to be. What I do expect to see is too horrible to dwell on, so I push it aside, concentrating instead on my receptionist. If this is affecting me, I can't imagine how Maxi is handling it. He's only Tramp's owner to me, but he's her big brother.

"I don't think he's in." Maxi's expression is a mix of fear

and disappointment. "What do we do now?" She looks to me for the answer, and I look at Don.

"I'm going to see if there's anyone on-site with a key."

Don's voice is decisive, and he leaves to do that. Maxi wraps her arms around her middle, gaze fixed on the floor. I put my hand out to touch her shoulder, but Marta gives me a quick shake of the head. She's the expert on younger humans, so I draw my hand back and fake a stretch to dispel the awkwardness. Marta gives me her patented eye roll and head shake combo, and I grin despite the somberness of the atmosphere.

Footsteps echo in the hallway behind us. Don and a tiny woman with a large bunch of keys are headed our way. Her clothes might be from now or fifty years ago, the skirt of her dress reaching almost to her ankles, belted tightly around a small waist. Combined with the knot of hair worn on the nape of her neck, she is the picture of everyone's grandmother. Or the scary housekeeper in a horror movie.

"Maxi, this is Mrs. Hendershott—did I get that right?—and she's the manager on-site." Don motions to Maxi, who automatically holds out a hand, but Mrs. H, as I'm already calling her, ignores the gesture. She focuses on the key ring, long fingers moving through a myriad of keys before she selects one. Opening the door, she silently motions for the four of us to follow her inside.

Marta's maternal instincts have already kicked in. She automatically reaches for Maxi, putting one arm about the girl's shoulders. She nods for me to follow Don, and I get the picture: she's going to keep Maxi back in case of the worst possible scenario.

And I'm glad she does this. What meets our eyes is chaos, pure and simple. I focus on the empty dog crate sitting on one corner of the living room. Where's Tramp? I push farther into the apartment, intent on finding what is probably a very frightened pup.

Of course, this might be the way Rex always lives, but my gut says otherwise. While the other three stand looking around the room, trying to decide on the next move, I continue through the apartment, my eyes peeled for a small dog.

I find him in the back bedroom, crouching under the unmade bed, mutely watching me as I extend a tentative hand for him to smell. He doesn't bark, which is a red flag to me. Something has terrified him so much it's made him retreat physically in more ways than one.

"Come on, pal," I say in a low voice, trying to coax him out. "I'm not going to hurt you."

To my relief, he begins moving slowly toward me, belly low to the ground and ears back. When he gets close enough for me to reach him, I put one hand underneath him and gently lift him out. He is trembling all over, from his stubby tail to his wet nose. I hold him close in both arms and let him nuzzle as I sit on the side of the bed.

"Hey, Marta, could you come here a sec, please?" I keep my voice low so I don't startle Tramp. I can hear Marta moving quickly toward the bedroom, leaving Maxi and Don with the key lady as they search the rest of the place.

"What's up?" Marta peeks around the edge of the doorway, her eyes widening slightly when she sees what I'm holding. "Is that the infamous Tramp?"

"Indeed it is," I agree, leaning down and brushing the furry head with my chin. "Any sign of his owner out there?"

Marta shakes her head, a worried expression on her face. "Not that we've seen so far."

"Oh, Dr. C, let me hold him," Maxi squeals, reaching out both hands for the little dog. He clearly recognizes her and gives her face a good wash with his soft pink tongue. I leave the two of them enjoying their reunion as Maxi mutters sweet nothings in Tramp's furry ears.

Don and Mrs. Hendershott are still standing in the front room, their heads close together as if sharing state secrets. When I walk in, they both turn to look at me.

"So, what's the verdict?" I ask. "Any sign of Rex?"

Don runs one hand over his thinning hair and shakes his head.

"Not so much as a peep, and Mrs. H. here says she hasn't seen him for almost two days." He glances down at the building manager, who nods vigorously, giving her an odd bobblehead doll appearance.

"Almost two days? Isn't that slightly odd?" I don't bother keeping the sarcasm quotient dialed down, and I'm almost glad to see Mrs. Hendershott flinch. "Or do people just come and go around here without anyone noticing?"

After giving the tiny woman a quick glance, Don speaks up in her defense. "Doc, be reasonable. First off, Rex is a grown man. Second, have you noticed how big this place is? How's anyone supposed to keep track of who's here and who isn't, not to mention take care of all the other issues?" His voice doesn't sound convincing, though. Maybe I'm supposed to magically understand something underlying his commentary. I take the plunge.

"Mrs. Hendershott, how many exits to the outside are there in this building?"

She pretends to think. When she speaks, I can see she's stalling for time. And hoping we haven't noticed.

"Two," she says. "The one you came through and one that leads to the back alley. Both are downstairs."

The import of her words takes a moment to sink in, but when it does, I'm beyond flabbergasted.

"So, this entire apartment building that houses, what, at least thirty people, only has two ways out in case of a fire? Or an earthquake?"

Don holds up both hands, palms facing me in a placatory gesture.

"Come on, Doc. You've seen how old this place is, right?" He pauses as if waiting for me to nod. I simply stare back at him. "Can you imagine how much it would cost to retrofit a place like this? The rent would be astronomical, not cheap like it is now."

"Oh, sure. That argument would totally fly with, say, the families of these lucky renters after a massive fire, wouldn't it? Not to mention their pets." I gesture behind me toward Rex's bedroom. "Tramp's not the only innocent animal who might be trapped in a place like this, waiting to be rescued."

"What's on fire?" Marta has come back into the living room, followed closely by Maxi and an ecstatic Tramp.

Don gives a forced laugh. "Me, if the doc here has her way." He clears his throat in the awkward silence that follows his comment, gaze fixed on Marta as if she alone can save him from this crazy woman standing just feet away.

And maybe he's right. When Marta turns to me, her eyes twinkling in amusement, I smile ruefully.

"Sorry, Don. I just get a bit carried away sometimes. Nothing personal." I hold out one hand to him. "Shake?"

His grasp is a bit tighter than needed. I take the hint.

"If there's no sign of Rex, we'd better give the police a call." Marta's voice is calm but commanding. She is moving into her take-charge mode, and I'm delighted to let her. I get too worked up when animals are concerned. I run my fingers through Tramp's fur and feel my blood pressure drop. Everyone needs an animal friend.

And right now, I'm wondering where Tramp's human friend might be. I sincerely hope nothing has happened to him. The way things are going lately, though, I'm not holding my breath.

Looking at Marta, I nod in agreement. It's time to call in the professionals.

CHAPTER SIXTEEN

T hanks for getting here so quickly."
Don steps forward to greet the two uniformed officers who join us in the foyer of the apartment building. Mrs. Hendershott has disappeared, probably to take care of another residential issue. Or to figure out how to explain the dearth of exit doors.

I, for once, am pleased to see our officers of the moment are both women. I know this seems both feminist and prejudicial, but my gut feeling—my womanly instinct—tells me this situation requires both intellect and intuition.

"You called in a missing person?" This is the younger-looking of the two, the one who seems barely old enough to purchase her own ammo. A hardness in her expression, though, tells me she is more than capable of handling anything from speeding tickets to physical takedowns.

"It's Rex," says Maxi, and the three of us let her give the particulars. He is, after all, her brother.

Held tightly in Marta's arms, Tramp gives a sharp bark at the mention of his owner's name. I reach over and give his soft ears a gentle tug. I can only imagine what he has seen.

Where is Dr. Doolittle when you need him?

"Will one of you show me the apartment?" The other

officer walks over to where I'm standing next to Marta. Her shoulders are twice the width of Don's, and when she crosses her arms, I can see the veins bulging near the surface. This is one tough gal.

"I can," offers our intrepid reporter, and I nearly laugh. He is incredibly transparent, our Don. Silently I wish him good luck at pumping this particular officer for anything other than a comment on the weather. Marta buries her face in Tramp's fur, hiding her smile.

Maxi has given up everything she knows about her brother's current situation and possible whereabouts. As the officer finishes writing up her notes, Maxi walks over to me and stands closely, swaying slightly. I can see how pale her face has become, and I catch her just as she begins another slow descent to the ground. Maybe she's not eating enough, I think. Maybe I'm not paying her enough to buy decent food. I make a mental note to check with Lou when I get back to clinic.

"Here, Gij, take the dog." Marta thrusts the squirming bundle of puppy at me and reaches for Maxi in one smooth gesture. Bending down beside the girl, she carefully positions her head on the tiled floor, waiting quietly for her to open her eyes.

Across the foyer, I can hear the footsteps of Don and Officer Buff Arms headed our way, neither one speaking. I can hardly wait to get him alone and interrogate him, find out what he dragged out of the officer. My guess is zilch, judging by his expression.

"Hey, is she all right?"

Don's irritation is quickly replaced with concern as he strides over to us. Maxi's eyes flutter open and then widen, and she struggles to sit up. Marta holds her in place, firmly but gently.

"She's fine," she says over her shoulder. "Just shock."

"Don't you think we need to call someone, maybe a doctor?" Don is looking at Maxi as Marta helps her stand, his head tilted in question.

Beside him, I snort. "I *am* a doctor, you numbskull. And I'm already here."

It's Don's turn to make a derisive sound. "Maybe if the little furry fella here needs some attention. I'm talking about a real doctor."

Thankfully, the officers interrupt us before I clock the idiot across his skull and make the news in a not so good way.

"Someone will be in touch," the younger-looking officer says, directing her comment to the four of us in general. Marta and I obediently nod in reply. Maxi, I notice, is leaning against Don's arm, but her color is definitely better. Don's, however, is something between bright pink and red. He really does need to cut out the ciggies and fast food; his blood pressure must be through the roof.

Of course, I might have helped it get there. The thought makes me grin, and he catches my eye, his own lips tightening into a thin line. I'd better play nice since he's our ride home. And I really don't want to be the subject of one of his in-depth investigative reports.

Silent for a moment, we watch the two officers walk out to their cruiser and pull out into traffic. Finally, Marta gives a small sigh and faces me, slipping an arm through mine.

"So, what's next?" She looks from me to the other two, head tilted to the side like an inquisitive bird. I lean down and impulsively plant a kiss on her cheek, earning a brilliant smile in return. At least one person still likes me.

Maxi shrugs, seemingly lost for words.

"Let's grab something to eat before we make another move," Don says as we head outside, nodding in mutual agreement. "I tell you what would make my day. Another round with Jinx."

Maxi stops walking, her eyes widening as she looks at him. "And what, exactly, does that mean?" She sounds suspicious, and I wait to hear how Don will explain himself to Jinx's sister.

"I, uh, met him the other day for an interview." Even though it's the truth, I sense a tinge of something else. Don is clearly treading water in a conversational pond he'd rather not be in right now. "Ask the doc here. She set it up."

"Indeed I did," I agree, giving Don a smile. "Set you up with Jinx, I mean."

"Not in that way," he protests, drawing the keys to the van out of his pocket and giving me a disgusted glance.

"What way is that, Don?" Marta poses her question with complete innocence, making me laugh while Don scowls. Purposefully turning his back on the three of us, Don climbs behind the steering wheel and closes the door with a bit more force than needed, rattling the glass.

Marta and I exchange an amused look, and Marta reaches out to pat Tramp's ears.

"We're just teasing, Maxi," she assures the girl. "Jinx was helping Don with a few things, that's all."

"And if you three women don't get a move on, I'll be having my next meal all by my lonesome."

With a semblance of peace restored, we decide on the nearest all-day breakfast joint, Mama J's Eggs 'n' More. Its interior is a mishmash of yellow gingham and blue stripes, an entire flock of hens parading around the room on shelves, the menus, and in various other guises.

"I don't think I've ever seen a chicken creamer before," Marta murmurs in my ear, and I almost laugh aloud.

"Want one?" I ask in a quasi-serious tone, and act as though I'm about to pocket said creamer, milk and all.

Marta gives my hand a playful slap. "Put that back right now, Gij, before they kick us out of here. I have no desire to bail you out of the pokey over a ceramic chicken."

Don's attention is drawn to someone behind me.

"Well, maybe not for a fake chicken, but how about a real one?"

He nods toward the door, and we all stare as Jinx walks in in all his campy glory, head swiveling as he peers around the café. When his gaze falls on our table, he pauses and then starts as if he's spotted the local bully. When he spins around to leave, I'm up and moving without even thinking about it.

"Not so fast there, Romeo," I say breezily, pulling him back against the building by his thin arm. "Not in the mood for a friendly chat? Our friend Don seems to think you led him a merry chase the other night, maybe not telling quite everything. Wanna talk about it?"

"No, I do not want to talk about it," he says as he tries to pull his arm away. "And why's my sister with you?"

"I think you need to come and find out for yourself, pal. Maybe we can exchange some real information, figure out where Rex might have disappeared to and things like that." I lean in closer, not caring my breath is more coffee than anything else. "Understand, rubber band?"

"Whatever."

His tone is sulky, but he follows me back inside. I motion at the server for another chair and push Jinx onto the bench seat next to Marta, taking the chair on the end for myself. I've boxed him in as easily as if I'd planned it. Maxi, sitting between Don and a low wall, just stares at her brother. And Jinx, I'm pleased to note, looks just this side of uncomfortable.

Looking over at Don, I nod. "Take it away," I say, ignoring Marta's amused shake of the head. "I think our friend here might have a few more things to tell us."

"About what?" His tone is sulky, but he knows exactly what I'm talking about, judging by the fact that he can't make eye contact with any of us.

"About your brother's whereabouts, for starters." Don leans forward across the table, and Jinx instinctively draws away from his intense blue gaze. "Any idea where Rex might be at the moment?"

"And Tramp's out in the van, J," Maxi breaks in, two bright spots of color on her thin cheeks. "He was all by himself, hiding under Rex's bed, like he was scared of something." Her voice is taut, as if she's trying to keep from crying. Marta, bless her motherly heart, reaches across the table and lays a hand on Maxi's clenched fists.

Jinx snorts, looking at Maxi.

"That dog is afraid of his own shadow, Max. Hiding is his thing."

Before anyone else can jump in and contribute to what's quickly becoming an emotional conversation, our server appears, a perky, high ponytail swinging behind her as she sashays up to our table.

"Welcome to Mama J's," she says, a slight drawl in her voice. I can't tell if it's real or not, but it's already charming Don. Of course. "Can I start y'all out with some hot coffee? And maybe a milk for you, miss?"

I glance at Maxi, my lips folded tightly to hold in my grin. But Miss Perky isn't talking to my receptionist. She's looking straight at Marta.

"That would be lovely," Marta says, shooting a quick smile at me. "And a water as well, if you don't mind."

"Not at all," says the server, shaking her head and sending

her ponytail into frenetic motion. "When I was expecting my little guy, that's all I wanted to drink."

"I'll take coffee, black," says Don, breaking into this maternal camaraderie. "And one for him as well," he says, jerking his chin at Jinx. Jinx says nothing, his eyes still fixed on the tabletop.

"I'll have an iced tea, no lemon." Maxi's face is back to its normal paleness, her irritation at her brother forgotten for the moment.

"And for you, ma'am?" The pen hovers above the bright yellow pad as she looks down at me.

Fabulous. I've been designated the old lady of the bunch. Ignoring Marta's amused expression—she knows how I feel about being labeled as "ma'am"—I ask for a Coke.

"And not diet, either. If I'm drinking the stuff, I want the real thing."

Without another word, she's off like a shot, giving Jinx a run for his money in serving style.

"So, back to what we were talking about," I say, giving Jinx a hard stare. Since his eyes are still angled downward, he misses my tough-gal stance. Marta, on the other hand, doesn't miss a thing. With a sigh, she leans over and puts an arm around Jinx's slight shoulders. We are the quintessential good cop, bad cop combo. I wonder if this will translate into our parenting style as well.

"Jinx, we think something might have happened to Rex, that he might not be safe." Her words are simple and have the desired effect. He looks up at her, worried. "Can you help us?"

Aha, I think. He *does* know something. I find myself leaning toward the two of them, eager to hear what he has to say. Don, on the other hand, has no such compunction.

"You can start by telling us what you know about this mess Rex is involved with," he says abruptly, and it shatters whatever connection Marta has begun to establish. I feel like kicking him under the table.

I am not known for curbing my impulses.

Shooting a scowl in my direction, he leans down to rub his shin. Maxi, I'm surprised to note, has to duck her head to hide a smile. It must be very entertaining for her to see her boss out in the wild like this. Hopefully, I won't end up on Facebook or Instagram or the latest social media platform.

"I don't know anything," Jinx blurts out more loudly than is polite. This garners our table a few curious glances, but that's it. This is San Francisco, after all. It's a city used to letting each person be herself, provided it doesn't shut down the BART or cause a traffic jam.

"I think you do." Maxi has finally joined the conversation, and her color is beginning to return. "Tell me what Rex was doing, Jinx. I know he talks to you more than he does to me."

Our drinks arrive, along with a few minutes of scrambling into the menus so we can order. Finally we are finished, and with another flip of her ponytail and a wide smile for Jinx, our server promises to "get this right in, y'all, and just holler if you need me."

Jinx nods, seemingly embarrassed to have been singled out. Maybe she's recognized a fellow inmate in the industry. Or maybe she's already pegged the rest of us as unworthy of her attention.

Don, I notice with amusement, is scowling down at the table. What must it be like to lose that fascination for the ladies? I sincerely hope I never have to experience that humiliation, my own lady included. Impulsively, I reach across the table and take Marta's hand, nearly upsetting Jinx's drink in the process. Marta smiles back at me and gives my hand a gentle squeeze.

"If you're done with all that lovey-dovey stuff, you two,

can we get on with what we were talking about?" Don's scowl has transferred itself to his voice. Marta, always concerned for the feelings of others, withdraws her hand and reaches for her drink instead.

I let my gaze rest on his just long enough to let him know I can read his thoughts, and then I face Jinx.

"So, back to what Marta asked you," I say, leaning back in the hard chair and crossing my arms over my chest. "What was Rex's part in all of this?"

"In all of what?" counters Jinx, his mouth set in a stubborn line. "I don't know what you're talking about." He glances around the table. "And that goes for all of you. As far I as know, he's just trying to make ends meet, like a lot of us."

I notice with interest he uses the present tense when speaking of his brother. He either knows where Rex is or he's incredibly naïve concerning everything that's occurred since that morning phone call from Chrissy Burton.

"Where is he?" Maxi's voice is soft, barely above a whisper. It has the desired effect on her brother, though, and he turns to face her. "Where is he?" she says again, and this time her voice is louder, more forceful.

We all face Jinx. He shrugs, but he's not as sure as he was just a moment ago. Something of the seriousness seems to be getting through. Finally.

"You really don't know where he's at?" Jinx sounds incredulous, his gaze shifting around the four of us. We all nod in agreement. "I swear I thought he was at his place."

"We've just come from there," I say.

"And we had to make a missing person report, and Tramp was hiding under the bed," Maxi says, her words coated with tears. "I'm scared, Jinx. I'm worried something bad has happened to him."

Don, to his credit and my surprise, leans over and gives

her shoulders an awkward side hug. Marta is already leaning across the table as far as her growing belly will allow, both hands reaching for hers. I can only sit and feel incredibly inadequate, silently vowing to give her a raise. It's the least I can do so she'll never have to sell her marrow or plasma or anything in order to make ends meet.

"Wait." Jinx holds out both hands, palms outward. "Are you guys saying Rex is missing? And you had to call the police?"

The four of us answer him with nods, a full complement of bobbleheads gathered around the table. When the waitress brings our food, we barely notice. Instead, all of us keep our gaze fully on Jinx as he digests our concern in silence.

"Well," he finally says, reaching for the spoon that juts from his Mama J's Sunrise Bowl of healthy goodness. "What Rex told me makes some sense, then." Taking a small bite of the fruit topping, he chews and swallows solemnly while I exchange a surprised look with Don and Marta. Maxi is sitting as if in a trance, her chin propped up on one hand, staring straight at her brother.

"Could you tell us what it was he said, Jinx?" Marta's voice is calm, but I know her well enough to see the rising excitement in her eyes.

Jinx shrugs. "I actually don't know if this has anything to do with where he's at right now, but he did happen to mention he was a little worried about someone. Not worried about them, but concerned about what they were doing."

"Did he give a name?" I can't help breaking into the exchange between him and Marta, my tone probably more strident than it needs to be. At the table next to us, I notice the occupants staring at me. I ignore them, focusing instead on Jinx.

"No, but something he said made me think it's Bev. You

know," he offers with a small grimace, "that woman who got knocked down in the parking lot at the Vineyard."

"Yeah, and she also happens to work with both Chrissy Burton and Marta," I can't help saying, a touch of acerbity in my words. "So if there's anything we need to know about her, Jinx, spit it out. Now."

"Give me a sec, all right?" His expression reminds me of a little boy who's been caught with one hand in the proverbial cookie jar while blaming someone else.

"I know what he said," says Maxi, and we all stare at her. She colors slightly under the scrutiny but lifts her chin and speaks. "Rex heard the organs are being sent to Syria. Something about being used for injured soldiers."

"For our soldiers?" I'm trying to process the idea organ donors are supplying overseas recipients when nothing has been said about that anywhere—not on the news, not online, and certainly not at the hospital.

Maxi shakes her head, her gaze fixed on mine. "No, not for our guys. For the others. The terrorists."

When I hear her say that last word, I am stunned. Beyond stunned, actually.

I am scared.

CHAPTER SEVENTEEN

"Where in the world did he hear that?"

Marta sounds as flabbergasted as I feel, and even Don's mouth is hanging open. Jinx, however, looks smug. He might as well have a neon sign above his head that says "I told you so."

Maxi's conversational bombshell is massive. So massive, in fact, I'm inclined to not believe her for a moment. It seems to me anything labeled as "terrorism" in our volatile society should be plastered all over the news. Still...

"So, Maxi, what I'm hearing you say is Rex discovered that the donor program is linked to terrorism?" Marta shakes her head slightly, a frown drawing her eyebrows together. "How come he knows this, but the program is still around? That doesn't make sense."

"I agree," I say, but my attention is focused on Don. I'm watching his face as he processes Maxi's announcement, his journalistic instinct locked into overdrive. "Don? What's your take?"

He sits silently for a moment, eyes fixed on his coffee mug. I'm startled to see just how sober his expression is. Don, it seems, is taking this seriously. That alone stirs my blood, kicks my heart into high gear. This must be how it feels to be on the cusp of a breaking story, and I can almost see why Don loves his career. Almost.

"If what you say is true, Maxi," he begins, his voice and words solemn, "your brother might have stumbled across something that will put his life in danger, if it hasn't already."

"Wait a sec. Hold up." Jinx lifts his hands, looking between Don and Maxi. "I thought he was just kidding, all right? Rex tends to get a bit melodramatic and likes to exaggerate the details."

"If this terrorism angle is true, or even just partway true, it's gonna blow the whole transplant program sky high." Don turns in his seat to face Maxi, his eyes serious. "Think carefully, okay? Where did Rex get all this information?"

I can't help it. I laugh. "So very sci-fi, Don. Organ transplants for wounded soldiers? Like a rebooted robot army?"

"Hey, I don't make the stories, I just report them, all right? And the more we learn about this, the better chance we'll have at finding Rex." Don's mouth tightens, and I can see that he's deadly serious. My heart takes a leap and settles back under my ribs, its rhythm shaking my chest like a tympani drum.

"So, how's the food?"

Our server has paused just behind me, her gaze skimming between the five of us, a fixed smile on her lips. She waits just a beat. "And here's your bill. No rush, now. Y'all enjoy your day." And she's off, swishing away to deposit a dose of faux country sweetness and a bill at another table.

"You know, Don, this whole conversation has kinda put a damper on the day." I'm trying for light, but it falls flat. Even Marta is still silent. "Okay, then. I'll take care of this and meet you guys at the van." I lean over and grab the bill, pushing the chair back with my knees. No one says anything, the mood somber and heavy. I sigh theatrically, catching Maxi's eye. "Having fun yet?"

"Gij, that's not necessary." Marta's tone is soft, but her words carry a warning to back off. I wrinkle my nose, but she ignores me.

"Fine," I mutter to myself, heading to the front counter. Gallows humor has always been my way of coping with stressful situations, but it's not everyone's cup of tea. I get that. I just wish that they'd get *me* for once.

Bill paid and back outside, I take in a deep breath of San Francisco air, enjoying the slight dampness that permeates everything here. On the warmer summer days, it can edge toward miserable, tropical even, but it's perfect today. I'm feeling a little better as I join the others at Don's van.

To my surprise, Jinx is coming with us. He climbs into the back seat behind Don, and Maxi climbs into the middle, an ecstatic Tramp jumping into her lap and giving her a series of wet kisses. Marta takes the seat behind me and I wait until she's buckled in, the belt adjusted across her middle, before I close her door and get into the front passenger seat. Looking over at Don, I wait to hear what the plan is.

"I vote we head back to Rex's apartment," he says. Don starts the motor, and we pull out into traffic behind a giant tour bus, the space between the two vehicles a mite closer than I would prefer. Don drives like he lives and works: too close to the edge for my taste. Gritting my teeth, I hang on and say nothing.

"Do you think he'll show up any time soon?" Jinx leans forward, his head jutting between the front seats. "I mean, it makes more sense he'd be at a friend's house or something, not at his place. That would make him a sitting duck, you know?"

"If he's really in some kind of trouble, certainly." I turn

to face him just as a motorcycle cuts down the center of the traffic, weaving his way between us and the neighboring SUV. Don lays on his horn, and the motorcycle rider gives us a one-fingered wave.

"What about the hospital?" Marta says, her voice steady. "Do you think he might there? Jinx, what do you think?"

Jinx leans back, shrugging. "I've got no clue, to be honest. I know he's scheduled to donate monthly. Blood plasma, I mean. I'm not sure when he last donated bone marrow."

We're all quiet for a moment, turning over possibilities in our minds. "Maxi, has Rex ever mentioned his donating schedule to you?" I say. What I really want to know is how the hospital deals with folks who've donated bone marrow. The other thing that Don mentioned, donating actual organs, I still can't get my head around that. It's just too Hollywood for me.

"No, not really." I watch her in the rearview mirror as she buries her face in Tramp's soft fur. "Well, he did tell me once he goes to that dog park to recruit."

"To recruit?" I think I already know the answer, but I want everyone else to hear it as well. "Do you mean to donate bone marrow? For money?"

Maxi nods. "Yes. Can you believe that woman even tried to rope me into it?"

"Bev?" Marta sounds dumbfounded. "She wanted you to donate? Are you even old enough, Maxi?"

"You only have to be eighteen and in good health. To tell you the truth, though, I'm not sure about that. I mean, how are all those junkies and winos in any shape to do that?"

I catch Marta's eye over the back of the seat. I know we're both thinking the same thing.

"So," I ask, "if someone can only donate bone marrow once, maybe twice, in a lifetime, how does Rex make his money?"

Maxi shrugs again, but Jinx, who has been staring out the window, speaks up.

"They get a kickback for each person they send to the clinic. You send enough people, you can make a decent wage."

"Wait. How in the world can a clinic afford that?" Don asks, glancing up into the rearview mirror. "Doc, make a note of that, if you would. I need to check that out ASAP."

I snort but do as he asks, typing a brief note into my phone. "What am I, your glorified copy girl?"

Behind me, Marta chuckles. "If you can get her to do anything besides worry about her precious animals, you've got some pull there, Don. God only knows how she'll deal with the baby when she or he gets here."

"Whatever, smarty. Speaking of which, who's going to keep Tramp until his daddy comes home?"

"He'll stay with me, right, Tramp?" Maxi's voice is muffled as she buries her face into the dog's fur. "And maybe he can come to work with me."

"Yeah, yeah, maybe. All we're missing is a ferret and a turtle."

"Can we get back to the donation clinic scheme thing?" Don's voice is impatient, but that might have something to do with the dense traffic around us. With the push to move to the surrounding bedroom communities such as San Leandro and Pleasanton, traffic in and out of the Bay Area can be a nightmare. "I think we need to find this Bev woman and have ourselves a little talk."

"Since I see her on a near-daily basis, Don, that won't be too difficult." Marta's voice is gentle, and I know she's unconsciously responding to the tension in him. "If you'd like, I can give her a call and set up a time for her to swing by our place. If that's okay with you, Gij." She reaches over the seat to give my shoulder a poke.

"Yeah, that's fine with me," I say, rubbing my shoulder in exaggerated pain. "Good God, woman. You need to cut those nails of yours."

"Just remember that next time you ask me to scratch your back," she says, but she sounds distracted. "Don, I just thought of something. Let's head back to our place right now. Gij, do you remember that internet issue Leif had?"

"You mean that dark web thingy? Tor?"

"That's it. Let's use my laptop and see if we can find anything about the clinic there."

"I'll make an investigative reporter out of you yet," says Don as he switches lanes and makes an abrupt left-hand turn, oblivious to the irate drivers and near misses behind us. He doesn't let any grass grow under his feet. And he doesn't use side mirrors, either.

❖

When the five of us are settled in the living room, Tramp dozing on Maxi's lap, Marta opens her laptop and begins searching for information.

"Okay, I'm in," she announces, eyes still fixed on the screen. "Any suggestions?"

"How about 'organs for sale'? That's pretty straightforward." Don looks around at the rest of us, one eyebrow lifted in question.

"Sounds good to me. Anyone want a coffee? Or tea?"

"Got any soda?" Jinx says. I can see the dark smudges under his eyes, proof he isn't sleeping because he's more worried than he's let on. "I'm talking the real thing, not that diet crap."

"Sure," I say without thinking and then glance guiltily over at Marta. She wants us to eat and drink stuff that will be a good example for the little one, but it's turned me into a sneak, to be honest. I keep my six-pack of Pepsi tucked behind the boxed foods in the pantry.

"Second shelf from the top, behind the gluten-free pasta," Marta says without taking her gaze from the screen. I can see the smile peeking out from the corner of her lips. "I had to move it to make room. And I'll take a bottle of water, please."

By the time I get back, everyone is watching Marta troll for any sign of an organ black market. It doesn't take long for her to find a promising site.

"Listen to this," she says, and I can hear the undertone of excitement in her voice. "'Prominent San Fran transplant hospital can procure the needed element.'" She looks up, her eyes shining with excitement. "Doesn't that sound as though they're saying they can get whatever you need for a transplant?"

Across the room, Don gives a half shrug, sipping carefully from an earthenware mug I'd gotten at some long-ago street fair. "Maybe. The only connection is the hospital's description, and it's tenuous." He holds up one hand, the other balancing the mug on his knee. "Just because this is from the part of the internet most folks don't ever see doesn't mean there's not an element of caution in what they post."

Marta's shoulders sag in disappointment. I slip an arm around her and drop a kiss on her hair.

"Sorry, love. I'm not saying you haven't found something already, but Don's right. These folks aren't going to wave their arms in the air and say 'over here.'"

"I know that," Marta says, indignant. "I just thought this sounded promising, all right?"

"I think it sounds damn good," Jinx says suddenly, and something in his voice makes the rest of us stare at him. He takes another drink from his glass, the ice cubes clinking. "I overheard Rex talking to Bev one night, and she was saying something about how a doctor and a couple RNs had joked about using the internet to drum up more business, maybe offer bone marrow and plasma to soldiers."

We sit silently for a moment, digesting Jinx's comments. Beside me Marta stirs, leaning closer to the laptop. I watch as she clicks on the link she's discovered, and I mentally cross my fingers that this won't send a posse of feds to our door. Maybe we should have called Leif first.

Don is the first one to speak.

"So, what I'm hearing you say is they suggested giving bone marrow and blood to the army?" His eyebrows are drawn close together as he thinks through this scenario. "I'm pretty sure the Red Cross handles that kind of stuff, Jinx."

Jinx shakes his head impatiently. "Not our army, idiot. They meant *other* soldiers, *other* armies." When we don't respond, he adds, "As in Syria. Get it?"

"Okaaay," Don says, the word drawn out, as if speaking slowly will help him gather his thoughts. He sets the mug down on the floor and leans forward, clasping his hands between his legs. "This is going to sound crazy, but just hear me out." He waits a moment, giving his words a gravitas that sends an involuntary shiver down my spine. "What if they're selling to terrorists?"

I give a derisive snort, moving my arm from around Marta as I reach over and sip from a can of Pepsi. "I'd ask what you've been smoking, Don, but I haven't seen any smoke so far."

"Just the plumes coming from his ears," murmurs Marta, and I have to laugh.

"I'm serious. Other countries have done the same thing, so why not the biggest capitalistic country on this planet?"

Marta and I exchange a glance, and I can see the disbelief

on her face. "Let's say for argument's sake you're right, Don," I begin, carefully placing the can of Pepsi back on the floor. "How could they—whoever they are—do this without being caught? I mean, surely someone is keeping track of donations and transplant needs and all that business, right?"

Don nods, and I notice the tense excitement in his posture and in the way his neck is jutting forward. He's a snapping turtle, eager to sink his teeth into something juicy.

"Of course. This is part of a legit operation—pardon the pun—and there are specific channels that have to be gone through."

"So? I'm still asking you how this could be done." I gesture to the laptop, noticing the slowly scrolling graphic at the top of the page.

"It could happen if the transplant team was in on it," Maxi says from her corner of the room, and I almost jump. I'd nearly forgotten she was there, and judging by the expressions on the others' faces, they had as well.

"Bingo, missy." Don points a nicotine-yellowed finger in her direction, a broad smile on his face. "You've got it in one."

Maxi's response is to snuggle closer with Tramp, who gives a yelp as she holds him a bit too tightly. The rest of us watch the pair of them, each keeping our thoughts private. I know my own mind is buzzing with Marta's possible discovery, but I'm also aware that Maxi and Jinx have a brother missing. If for no other reason, we need to figure out what is going on here and quickly.

"Personally," begins Jinx, his voice hesitant, "I think we need to call the PD, let them know what we've found." I hear Maxi's derisive snort and have to smile. "I'm serious, Max. If someone has Rex, we need to get the police involved, not try to go all Nancy Drew here." Jinx slumps back in his chair. "I'm just saying, okay?"

"And I'm just saying that it's hilarious coming from you, Mr.-I-Like-My-Weed. Since when are you a fan of the police?" Maxi's eyebrows are lifted as high as they'll go, giving her normally smooth forehead a corrugated appearance. "But as it happens, I agree with you for once." She turns to me, and I can see the toll this morning has taken on her. "Doc, don't you think we should call them?"

"Actually," Marta says in a gentle voice, "I think we need to get the bigger guns in for this one."

"Bigger guns?" I think I know what she means, but I want the others to hear it as well.

Marta nods. "Since this seems to involve something potentially international, I'm suggesting we contact the local FBI office."

I know Don's imagining the story going viral, his byline firmly printed above the headlines. Still, I have no desire to get on the bad side of the feebs with our digging into the dark web. Doing time in a federal prison for meddling isn't exactly my idea of a vacation from work. Of course, my imagination is usually bigger than the actual outcome, but I prefer life on *this* side of the bars, thank you very much.

We decide Marta is the best one to make the call. And as the rest of us listen to her voice as she describes what may be happening in one of the Bay Area's largest and most respected hospitals, a shiver trips down my spine.

It all boils down to a dead woman floating in the bay.

CHAPTER EIGHTEEN

I watch the three agents who show up at my house, noting each one seems to be doing something different than the others. One is asking questions of us all while the only woman in the trio, a short blonde with a blood-red manicure, taps notes into a tablet. The sound her nails make as they move across the screen is almost hypnotic, a staccato rhythm as she records our words.

The third member of the group, the older of the two men, is simply listening to each of us speak, his expression neutral but intense. I get the feeling he will be able to repeat each statement verbatim once they leave. Marta seems to have that skill as well. She can recall and repeat any and all of the goofy things I've ever said, no matter how long ago it was.

Thinking about that almost makes me smile, and I catch the eye of the agent taking notes. It's as if my thoughts have suddenly exposed themselves in one of those comic strip bubbles. I instantly rein in my amusement and tie it down firmly. This is a serious matter.

Satisfied I'm once again displaying the somberness equal to the situation, she turns back to the tablet. Never let it be said I don't believe in the ability of women to read the vibes of others. I've lived with Marta too long to ignore it. Our kid is going to believe in it as well, once she or he hits the uncertainty of puberty. There will be no secrets, nothing hidden from Marta, and I can hardly wait to see her in action.

I almost smile again.

When the five of us have given up everything we've discovered, the three agents exchange a few looks and nods, apparently able to communicate via telepathy. I'm watching them with interest and notice Jinx is as well. Maxi's face is once again buried in Tramp's fur, and Don is making his own notes in a battered spiral notebook, the quintessential journalist. Marta, as usual, is sitting still, but she has an awareness about her as if she's taking a reading from the room's atmosphere. Maybe she is. Her training as a social worker would have taught her how to read others' actions as clearly as if they had spoken their intentions out loud.

I can't stay still. I get to my feet, gesturing to Don and the two men.

"Anyone want a top-off? Don?" The two agents shake their heads, but Don answers with a relieved look in his eyes. The man could probably live on coffee and cigarettes.

"Sure," he says, holding the cup toward me with his left hand and still writing with the other. "And could you add some water to it this time? That first cup was strong enough to walk around by itself."

"Sissy," I say, smiling sweetly. He scowls in return, and I catch a fleeting smile on Maxi's face as I turn away and head for the kitchen. I'm glad. I've been worrying about her, especially since her fainting episode earlier in the day. She's got an armful of furry medicine, though. I'm glad Tramp is there.

When Don has his refill and I'm seated once more beside Marta, the agent who asked the questions stands, and the other two follow suit.

"Well, folks, I think that's it for now. We'll take this

information back to the office and get right on it, get a missing person case started. And, Don? Let's keep it out of the papers for the time being, all right? I'll let you know when it's acceptable to release the information."

Don gives a small nod, but I can tell he's irritated. I don't blame him. Sitting on a huge story, especially one with possible international scope, has got to be torture for an investigative journalist. Don doesn't seem to be a model of forbearance to begin with, and now he's being forced to act accordingly. Great. He'll be a bundle of fun to be around.

After the agents have gone, I suggest calling out for pizza for the five of us. Marta shakes her head, her gaze fixed on something in the distance that probably isn't there, something that's on her mind. Maxi keeps her face down, resting against a very patient Tramp. Don is still scribbling away in his notebook, and Jinx is the only one who speaks up.

"If it's all right with you guys, I need to go home. Max? How about you? Are you ready to hit the road?"

"Yes," is the muffled reply. "Doc, if it's okay with you, I really want to head home. I can text Akemi, check to see if she's cool with staying until the clinic closes today."

"Fine," I say, giving Maxi a smile. "Marta, you want to come with me to take these two home?"

"I'll do it." Don's gruff voice cuts across the room as he flips his notebook closed, tucking it back in his pocket. "Doc, let me know if you hear anything else." He stands, motioning to Jinx and Maxi to follow him.

I wrinkle my forehead in response. I'm not sure what he thinks I'll hear, especially since Chrissy Burton seems to be AWOL, and Bev Strait is currently nowhere to be found. Still, I just nod, suddenly wanting to be alone with Marta. But when our front doorbell rings, I know our quiet afternoon is at an end.

Chrissy Burton stands there, a vaguely wild look about her. I've never seen her without her hair perfectly arranged or her clothes anything but stylish and immaculate. The woman standing at my door looks as though she's been dragged through a bramble bush backward, to use my granny's words.

"Can I come in?"

I realize I'm staring and quickly step aside, motioning for her to follow me in to the living room.

"Can I get you something to drink?" I ask, sending Marta a silent message with my intense stare. She telegraphs one back: something is very wrong here. I get that just by looking at Chrissy.

"Coffee is fine." She sinks into the armchair earlier occupied by Maxi, and her nose twitches. "Do you have a dog?"

Something causes me to hedge my answer, give only a partial truth. She must be smelling Tramp. Rex's dog.

"I probably carry home a ton of pet hair on a daily basis," I say, giving her what I hope is a sincere smile. "Hazards of the job, so to speak."

Chrissy's answer is a sneeze.

Marta hands her a mug of coffee and sits beside me. She turns so that her back is against my side and her legs are stretched out along the couch, both hands clasped over her belly. Looking across at Chrissy, she says, "We've been a bit worried about you lately. Is everything okay? I mean, I know it's not really, but how are you doing?"

Chrissy shrugs, taking a sip of her coffee and sinking back against the chair's cushions. A small sigh escapes her, and it strikes me she is acting like a woman who's been rushing around, trying to get a lot of things done at once. She has that air about her, an impression of the rock that's gathering no moss. I wonder what's kept her so frenetically occupied.

It doesn't take long to find out. Everything about Rex. Bev. Even a hint concerning the woman in the water.

Afterward, I wish I'd just let it go, let the feds handle it without my input. The only thing that I do that shows any common sense is to text Don. For some reason I feel the need to tell him who's in my house. And that she wants to show me and Marta something, something near the bay.

"I'll drive," I volunteer. "Marta, don't you think you need to stay here? Maybe keep your feet up for a while?" I don't want her going anywhere with this potentially crazy woman, even if I'm there. And to be honest, I have no idea why I've agreed to go. Maybe I'm harboring some secret Sam Spade fantasy, where I manage to find the last clue that ties everything together.

"Nope." Marta is firm in her reply. "If you go, I go. Besides, Chrissy seems as though she could use the company right now."

As we're belting into the Honda's seats, I take out my cell phone once more and quickly tap out another text to Don: *heading to Pier 45. M and C with me.* I include an emoji with its eyes opened wide. Hopefully mine will be as well. The atmosphere in the SUV is slightly off-kilter, and all my senses are on high alert.

❖

By the time we arrive at the pier, I realize Marta and I have probably just made one of the dumbest decisions in our lives. Chrissy has gotten very, very quiet, and when I peek into the rearview mirror, she's got one hand on her waistband. That's never a good sign, at least in all the movies I've seen over the years.

"Stop," she says suddenly, pointing to a parking lot on the

deserted end of the pier. I obey, turning the Honda sharply as Marta falls against the door. When I've pulled into a parking space, I look around and realize that we've driven behind one of the Bay Area's finest hospitals, known for its child cancer ward. And transplants. When I glance at Marta, I can see she's realized it as well. We open our doors and step out onto the dull black tarmac. Chrissy does the same. And when I face her, I see something I'll have a hard time forgetting, if indeed I ever do.

To say Chrissy Burton's face is distorted with rage is to put it mildly. Not a conventionally pretty person to begin with, right now she is absolutely incandescent with anger, and the snarl on her mouth is just this side of feral.

"You two," she snaps, biting off each word cleanly as she glares at us. "You just couldn't leave well enough alone, could you?" The gun is pointing straight at us, her knuckles white as she grasps it tightly. I try to see if the safety is on without being obvious I'm looking, but I can't tell from where Marta and I are huddled against the tire well.

Marta's body trembles against me; her arms are wrapped protectively around her stomach. Without thinking my action through, I thrust her behind me and stand tall, hands planted on my hips, matching Chrissy's glare with one of my own. You mess with *mi familia*, you mess with me.

"Look, Chrissy, it's over, so you might as well put that thing down." I nod toward the pistol, amazed to find my chin is not quivering. Maybe I'm tougher than I thought. Or maybe I'm still in shock at who is holding a gun on me. Of all the suspects on the list, Chrissy's name would have never made an appearance. After all, wasn't she the victim here?

And just like that, a light bulb goes off. Taking in a deep breath, I lower my hands to my sides, palms facing her in a sign of placation.

"Chrissy," I begin, my eyes fixed firmly on hers and not on the gun swiveled in my direction, "who do you blame the most? Was it the doctors? Your parents? Who was it?"

I really don't know what I'm talking about, but she does. Her eyes widen and her arm lowers just a smidgeon. This entire thing has been about Chrissy seeing herself as a victim. And since it seems to be centered on the transplant she endured as a child, I assume that's what she's thinking about right now.

"You have no idea what it was like to watch your best friend get sicker and sicker." She spits the words at me, gesturing with the pistol. Behind me, I can hear Marta's muted intake of breath.

"Hey, do you think you could put that down for a few minutes?" I nod at the gun. "I really want to hear what you have to say, but to be perfectly honest, that thing is taking all my attention." I let myself smile slightly, hopefully showing Chrissy I don't mean anything offensive. The last thing I want to do is upset her.

To my relief, she glances at the hand holding the gun almost as if she's surprised to see it there. Without a word, she tucks it into the waistband of her jeans, and I hear Marta let out a long sigh.

"Thanks," I say, and I mean it from the bottom of my frenetically thumping heart. "Tell us about your best friend, Chrissy. What was her name?"

"Her name was Anika," she says in a quieter voice. "Anika Petrofsky, and she was my age, just eight years old. Can you imagine knowing you're going to die when you're that little? Can you?" I can't, and she doesn't give me time to respond. "And she was going to die because her family didn't have the money to move up the transplant list like mine did." Chrissy Burton stares directly at me, her eyes filled with tears. "They came to this damn country, to San Francisco, because they'd heard kids with leukemia were always taken care of, were always cured. They spent every dime they had to get here, and when they did, it was to find out about that damn transplant list."

The three of us are silent for a moment, and then I hear Marta getting slowly to her feet. When she moves around me, I reach for her but she shrugs out of my grasp and walks over to stand just in front of her boss. And the gun.

"Chrissy," she begins softly, "I'm so sorry about Anika, I really am. I wish you would have told me sooner."

"Yeah? And what could you have done about it?" The response is automatic, but she's trying hard not to break down.

"Honestly? I don't know." Marta places one hand gently on Chrissy's arm. "But I would have made damn sure no one else's child would have to suffer like she did." She moves her other hand to her belly, letting it rest there. "And I'd make damn sure no one would do that to my baby if she needed a lifesaving procedure. Money should never matter in situations like this."

Chrissy snorts, swiping at her eyes with the back of one hand. "It sounds good to say it now, but when you're just a kid, no one listens to you."

"Did you know about the list?" Marta's voice is quiet, and I stand listening, my entire body waiting for the answer.

Chrissy nods. "Sometimes the nurses would talk in front of us, as if they thought we weren't listening or wouldn't understand. I tried to tell my mom, but she'd always hush me and tell me not to worry about things that shouldn't concern me. Looking back, I suppose it was her way of telling me to be happy I was getting the treatment I needed and not to worry about anyone else." She shakes her head, and when she speaks again, her voice is imbued with bitterness. "After all, she had my dad and my brother and me to care for, and she wasn't going to use her energy on anyone else."

"You know, Chrissy," I say without thinking, "your mom was probably exhausted out of her skull. Dividing herself among three other people who needed her, as you said, and having no time for herself can make anyone selfish."

"But Anika was only a little girl!"

The wail that comes from her mouth absolutely tears me apart. How many years had she carried this hurt, this guilt? To be honest, it's amazing she hasn't struck out before now. Marta instinctively leans into her boss and envelops her in a hug.

I decide to take a page from Don Butler's investigative book as I slowly, silently slip my cell phone out of my back pocket. Chrissy's gaze is fixed on Marta's face now, but I don't think she's seeing anything except her memories. With a quick glance down at the screen, I select the recorder icon with one thumb, nudging the speaker's volume up as far as it will go before replacing the phone in my pocket, careful to keep the mouthpiece facing upward. I can only hope she'll say something that will help solve the mystery of the woman in the bay and Rex's disappearance.

Marta moves back from Chrissy, reaching around and rubbing her lower back. She grimaces slightly, and I'm instantly concerned she might be in pain. Instead, she simply smiles at Chrissy and asks if we can sit someplace for a while. Talk about panache.

"Here," I say, reaching over to open the Honda's back door. "Sit here, love. I can stand."

I wait for Chrissy to start waving that ridiculous gun around again, but she doesn't. Marta sinks into the back passenger seat with a little groan, but she waves me off when I lean toward her.

"Just my body trying to make room for this little one," she says, patting her tummy in that now-familiar gesture. "Only growing pains." She looks at Chrissy. "I'm glad you told us about your friend. Can you explain why Rex and that other woman had to die, though? Did they have something to do with Anika's death?"

I'm damned if I can see any ties from the past that link the two deaths to Anika Petrofsky, but Chrissy is clearly anxious to tell us all about it.

"That woman was a fluke, to be honest. I'd gone to the hospital for my annual check-in and there she was, gossiping with another woman about her new job, donating bone marrow and being paid to recruit new donors. I just saw red. Every time I had to go there, I thought about Anika, about how lucky I'd been and how unfair her life was. Hearing that someone was still using the sick as a way to make money made me furious." She pauses, thinking.

"And then what happened?"

Chrissy shrugs. "I was already finished with my appointment, so I just followed her down to the pier. All I wanted to do was to tell her how horrible it was to be on the other end of the bone marrow scheme, but she didn't give me a chance. Instead, she actually had the gall to tell me about 'this cool way to make some extra cash,' and I just lost it."

"So, how did she end up with your appointment card?" I can't help asking the question, but I also want her answer for the recording.

Chrissy gives a short, mirthless laugh. "I shoved it in her face, told her I was a childhood leukemia survivor. She grabbed it from me so she could see it better, I suppose. When she pocketed it, telling me I should be grateful for people like her and she was going to report me for harassment, I just gave her a shove."

She looks down briefly as if still seeing the woman's body. "I guess she hit her head on one of those concrete barriers they've put on the pier. I just gave her another push with my foot and in she went, simple as that. To say I was shocked when they ID'd her as me—well, that was pure irony as its finest." She gives a small smile. "And Rex was collateral damage. Wrong place, wrong time, I guess you might say. When I went to his apartment to confront Bev over her role in the donate-for-money scheme, he was there. And since I'd come to put an end to his income, he decided to put up a fight." She laughs. "It wasn't much of one, really. You know what they say about bringing a knife to a gun fight." She reaches down and gives the pistol an almost fond pat.

"So, why ask me to help you in all this?" I'm beyond stumped, trying to make sense of it all.

This time her laughter is genuine.

"Because I thought if there was any loose end, you'd be able to find it and give me the chance to finish cleaning up. Thanks for the info on Bev, by the way. I never did like that woman."

Marta and I just stare at her. I'm trying to come to grips with this living conundrum standing here in front of me. She is fiercely protective of the children her office is responsible for, and maybe now I can see why. But where does this cold-blooded instinct come from? Can the same person casually take two lives and still be an advocate for others' welfare? I have to give my head a small shake as I attempt to sort it all out.

Chrissy, however, has other ideas.

"Well, this conversation has been nice, but it isn't going to solve the current issue, is it?" To my dismay, she's withdrawn the pistol again. "There's still someone else who needs to face the music."

I can't help it. I ask who it is.

The laughter issuing from Chrissy's twisted mouth is just this side of maniacal, and it reminds me of those crazy horror films set in a forest cabin or an abandoned amusement park. Just before the madman—or madwoman—raises the knife or machete. Or gun.

The sound of the shot is almost deafening. I stand with my eyes closed, both hands clapped tightly against my ears. I suppose I'm waiting for the sting of the bullet, but instead I feel nothing, and my eyes pop open as a sickly thought dawns on me. Marta. The baby.

But Marta is still standing there, one hand covering her mouth and her horrified eyes peering over it. The very still form of Chrissy Burton lies crumped at her feet, limp fingers still clutching the gun. I'm surprised I don't see any blood.

"You gals all right?"

Don Butler steps from somewhere behind me, and I watch in an almost dreamlike state as he slips a small black pistol back into the holster that hangs from one hip, and then he reaches down to gently remove its twin from Chrissy's now-slack hand.

Holding out an ancient flip phone in our direction, he says, "If one of you will call for an ambulance and the police, I'll make sure Ms. Burton here is all right."

Marta, thank goodness, has the presence of mind to place the call. I'm still trying to process the fact that Chrissy is now moving on the ground, struggling to sit upright. Don, however, keeps her in place with one hand placed firmly on her shoulder.

"Am I dead?"

I want to laugh at the absurdity of the question. Don grins at me and then squats down next to a clearly confused Chrissy.

"No, ma'am, you sure aren't. I shot into the air and you fainted, plain and simple." He looks over at Marta, who's still on the phone, giving the emergency dispatch operator directions to where we are. "And as soon as help gets here and these two ladies have had a chance to give their story to the police, I'm taking them home."

Instead of protesting as I thought she might, Chrissy just closes her eyes. It occurs to me this has been her response to everything in her life, from the death of her friend to the various crimes she's committed in order to bring attention to the bigger crime of the transplant black market. A worthy message delivered in the worst way possible.

It's all about choices.

The Oakland Police Department arrives in all its glory, sirens blaring and lights flashing. Chrissy still doesn't open her eyes, and I wonder if she's gone catatonic or whatever people do when they're in shock. Or about to face reality. I don't have too long to worry about her, though.

Marta and I are hustled over to a pair of officers who separate us and take our statements. I'm not fully comfortable with that, to be honest, but I've seen enough live police shows to know this is how it's done. I tell it all, from meeting up with Chrissy earlier in the evening to the dramatic revelations to the arrival of Don Butler. The officer gives a small grunt when I give his name, and I remember most of the police departments in the Bay Area probably know his name. He's quite the pot stirrer at times.

And he's going to be absolutely insufferable after this. He must have a hidden wish of being the cowboy in the white hat, riding in to save the fair maiden—or maidens, in this case— and riding off into the sunset with a jaunty wave of his hand.

And I have never been happier to let someone live his dream. I'd hate to think what might have happened, how things might have turned out, if he hadn't ridden into town. I might even buy him that white hat.

EPILOGUE

When it comes down to it, Chrissy Burton's heart was in the right place. She was frustrated, angry at a system that had allowed such lax oversight for something that should have been held in highest esteem, not for the highest bidder. But it's never right to take a life for a life. Some may argue with me and say that's exactly what needs to be done in order to shut down these human black markets. It does make me wonder if we are as civilized, as advanced as we claim to be.

Thanks to Chrissy's ultimate confession—and with a little help from my unauthorized recording—the entire conduit for selling bone marrow to those desperate enough to pay has been shut down. The well-known transplant surgeon Dr. Anita Mericello has been charged with trafficking in human organs, along with three of the oncology nurses and two consultants. When their various Mercedes and Range Rovers and McMansions were confiscated, the news knocked even the latest political fiasco off the top ten.

Bev Strait is back at work at the county social services department. Unfortunately, she seems to have escaped unscathed from this whole bone marrow selling scheme. In our state, along with a handful of others, it's not illegal to sell one's bone marrow. Still, I like to think her reputation is tainted now and she'll take the hint and leave. The idea of

Marta having to see her on a regular basis is enough to make my blood boil, to put it mildly.

Maxi and Jinx seem to be doing well, considering they lost their brother. Tramp has moved in with Maxi and comes to work with her several days a week, and I'm glad. It means she has something else to focus on, something to keep her tied to the living and the present.

Jinx? Well, he's back to doing what he does best: smiling and twirling and flirting with the customers at the Vineyard. Marta and I still go there occasionally, both to enjoy the ambience and to keep an eye on the boy. As Marta commented recently, we tend to gravitate to those who are needy and hurting. Our tribe is filled with those in need of a lifeline.

Don Butler, to my amazement and Marta's amusement, has taken to swinging by for the odd coffee or beer. I have to admit, although I'll never say it aloud, he's not that bad a person, at least for a journalist. When he jokes about being the little one's unofficial "god-daddy," I just laugh. Who knows, though? Stranger things have happened.

As for Chrissy Burton, she is currently residing in the state psychiatric hospital. With her medical history and the results of a mental evaluation, it was deemed prudent to commit her both involuntarily and indefinitely. Whether or not she'll ever face murder charges remains to be seen. Personally, I hope she gets the help she needs. Living with that awful burden would be enough to make anyone lose their grip on reality.

Speaking of needing some help, today is The Day, capital letters included. I've faced down snarling dogs before without flinching. I know there's nothing wrong with my mettle. I've handled plenty of situations that require nerves of steel. But this is an entirely different kettle of fish. A horse of a different color. A baby.

"Okay, missy," begins the cheerful technician as she helps

Marta onto the exam table. "Just get comfortable and lift your shirt for me."

She bustles around the small room, clicking on a computer and getting gel down from a cabinet. I wink at Marta as she raises the voluminous maternity top. I'm rewarded with a classic eye roll.

The sight of the mound that is her stomach makes something clench in mine. This is real life. There is no going back now, even if I wanted to. I scoot around to the other side of the table and sit down on a stool that almost rolls out from beneath my suddenly unsteady legs. The idea that we are about to get our first glimpse of our child has me almost in panic mode.

"Ready?" The technician beams down at Marta and gives me a cursory glance. We both nod, and I reach for Marta's hand. Hang on tight, I say silently, and I'm unsure if that was meant for me or Marta, who, quite honestly, is as cool as a cucumber, her hand smooth and dry under my damp one.

"This might be a little cold," she says, and we're off. For the next few minutes I barely breathe as I watch the wand trace a course across Marta's belly. There is the sound of clicking as the tech records what she is seeing, but my eyes are glued to the screen. I've had plenty of experience with ultrasounds before in the clinic, so the various vague blobs and shapes I'm seeing have started my heart racing. I glance down at Marta, curious to see her reaction to the gray and white mass, and I wonder if she's already aware of what the three of us are now staring at.

"Here's baby one, gals, and here's baby two." The technician grins down at Marta and over at me. "Congrats. You're having twins."

God bless Mr. Flores. He really should set up a baby prediction business.

I'm already reaching for Marta, tears rolling unheeded down my cheeks. Fumbling in my back pocket for the small velveteen box I've been carrying for a while now, I pull it out and open it with shaking fingers.

"Marta Perry," I say as I stare into her tear-filled eyes and slip the diamond solitaire onto her slightly swollen finger, "would you do me the immense honor of marrying me?"

About the Author

Ellie Hart is a lifelong writer whose love of mysteries was formed early in life. At age eight, she discovered Agatha Christie—much to her mother's dismay—and began devouring any and all books she could find that featured murder and mayhem. After a twenty-year career as a high school and community college English teacher, she now devotes her newly found freedom to writing mystery novels and reading for pleasure. Ellie lives in the Sonoran Desert and dreams of moving to a place where the seasons are something besides hot and hotter.

Books Available From Bold Strokes Books

Comrade Cowgirl by Yolanda Wallace. When cattle rancher Laramie Bowman accepts a lucrative job offer far from home, will her heart end up getting lost in translation? (978-1-63555-375-8)

Double Vision by Ellie Hart. When her cell phone rings, Giselle Cutler answers it—and finds herself speaking to a dead woman. (978-1-63555-385-7)

Inheritors of Chaos by Barbara Ann Wright. As factions splinter and reunite, will anyone survive the final showdown between gods and mortals on an alien world? (978-1-63555-294-2)

Love on Lavender Lane by Karis Walsh. Accompanied by the buzz of honeybees and the scent of lavender, Paige and Kassidy must find a way to compromise on their approach to business if they want to save Lavender Lane Farm—and find a way to make room for love along the way. (978-1-63555-286-7)

Spinning Tales by Brey Willows. When the fairy tale begins to unravel and villains are on the loose, will Maggie and Kody be able to spin a new tale? (978-1-63555-314-7)

The Do-Over by Georgia Beers. Bella Hunt has made a good life for herself and put the past behind her. But when the bane of her high school existence shows up for Bella's class on conflict resolution, the last thing they expect is to fall in love. (978-1-63555-393-2)

What Happens When by Samantha Boyette. For Molly Kennan, senior year is already an epic disaster, and falling for mysterious waitress Zia is about to make life a whole lot worse. (978-1-63555-408-3)

Wooing the Farmer by Jenny Frame. When fiercely independent modern socialite Penelope Huntingdon-Stewart and traditional country farmer Sam McQuade meet, trusting their hearts is harder than it looks. (978-1-63555-381-9)

Shut Up and Kiss Me by Julie Cannon. What better way to spend two weeks of hell in paradise than in the company of a hot, sexy woman? (978-1-163555-343-7)

Spencer's Cove by Missouri Vaun. When Foster Owen and Abigail Spencer meet, they uncover a story of lives adrift, loves lost, and true love found. (978-1-163555-171-6)

Unexpected Lightning by Cass Sellars. Lightning strikes once more when Sydney and Parker fight a dangerous stranger who threatens the peace they both desperately want. (978-1-163555-276-8)

Without Pretense by TJ Thomas. After living for decades hiding from the truth, can Ava learn to trust Bianca with her secrets and her heart? (978-1-163555-173-0)

Emily's Art and Soul by Joy Argento. When Emily meets Andi Marino she thinks she's found a new best friend, but Emily doesn't know that Andi is fast falling in love with her. Caught up in exploring her sexuality, will Emily see the only woman she needs is right in front of her? (978-1-163555-355-0)

Escape to Pleasure: Lesbian Travel Erotica, edited by Sandy Lowe and Victoria Villaseñor. Join these award-winning authors as they explore the sensual side of erotic lesbian travel. (978-1-163555-339-0)

Ordinary is Perfect by D. Jackson Leigh. Atlanta marketing superstar Autumn Swan's life derails when she inherits a country home, a child, and a very interesting neighbor. (978-1-163555-280-5)

Royal Court by Jenny Frame. When royal dresser Holly Weaver's passionate personality begins to melt Royal Marine Captain Quincy's icy heart, will Holly be ready for what she exposes beneath? (978-1-163555-290-4)

Strings Attached by Holly Stratimore. Rock star Nikki Razer always gets what she wants, but when she falls for Drew McNally, a music teacher who won't date celebrities, can she convince Drew she's worth the risk? (978-1-163555-347-5)

Answering the Call by Ali Vali. Detective Sept Savoie returns to the streets of New Orleans, as do the dead bodies from ritualistic killings, and she does everything in her power to bring their killers to justice while trying to keep her partner, Keegan Blanchard, safe. (978-1-163555-050-4)

Lightning Source UK Ltd.
Milton Keynes UK
UKHW040605020419

340345UK00001B/57/P

DOUBLE VISION

By the Author

The Deep End

Double Vision